A SCANDALOUS MIDNIGHT IN MADRID

SUSAN STEPHENS

MILLS & BOON

First published in Great Britain 2019
by Mills & Boon, an imprint of HarperCollins*Publishers*
1 London Bridge Street, London, SE1 9GF

Large Print edition 2019

© 2019 Susan Stephens

ISBN: 978-0-263-08286-9

MIX
Paper from
responsible sources
FSC C007454

This book is produced from independently certified FSC™ paper to ensure responsible forest management. For more information visit www.harpercollins.co.uk/green.

Printed and bound in Great Britain
by CPI Group (UK) Ltd, Croydon, CR0 4YY

For my wonderful readers,
who support and enthuse me
more than they know.
Thank you. xx

CHAPTER ONE

THE SKY WAS as deep and smooth as black velvet over the heart of old Madrid, as Don Alejandro, Duque de Alegon unfolded his powerful frame from a vehicle he'd casually abandoned outside the hottest club in town. City clocks chimed midnight as a valet rushed to park the top-of-the-range muscle car. Nightlife in Spain's capital was fast and furious… and late.

Pressing a generous tip into the attendant's hand, Alejandro switched his attention to a flash of flame on the opposite side of the street, where, framed in harsh light, a woman was flambéing a dish alongside the world-renowned Chef Sorollo in the kitchens of El Gato Feroz. The young woman was voluptuous beneath severe chef's whites, her mouth was firm and her brow was furrowed with concentration. Her attention didn't waver from the task as her small, capable hands worked swiftly to some internal rhythm.

As if sensing she was being observed, she glanced up. Distance stole the details, but her glance was sharp and bright with intelligence, and he guessed there'd be a sprinkling of freckles across her short, straight nose, as a few baby curls of copper-bright hair had escaped the cap she wore for work. Fiery hair was reputed to mean a fiery demeanour, which led to thoughts of fire in his bed. He could vouch for the food she was preparing being exceptional, as he had dined at El Gato Feroz many times. That was the reason he'd chosen the restaurant to host his sister's engagement party tomorrow night, and why he was here, outside the club where his sister was holding a pre-engagement party for her female friends. Her last night of freedom, as Annalisa had worryingly told him.

'Alejandro!' his sister yelled now.

He held up a restraining hand, impatient to see more of the woman in the kitchen. What was it about the young chef that gripped his interest, when beauties and sophisticates of every type were waiting inside the indigo womb of Club Magia? Something about her confident demeanour chimed with his approach to life, Alejandro decided. Here in Madrid, he was Don Alejandro de Alegon, a Spanish grandee of impeccable lineage with responsibilities and duties that embraced an international business, as well as vast land holdings and a wayward sister, but when he left the city he was a different man. It was the poise of the woman that suggested she could adapt as easily as he could that made him curious to know if there was some other side of the young chef with the serious demeanour.

'Alejandro!' Annalisa repeated with frustration. 'My friends are waiting to meet you.'

All the more reason for delay. 'I'll be there in a few minutes,' he promised as he turned to cross the street.

Annalisa's friends were in no danger from him. His taste ran to older women who knew the score. No long-term entanglements. No complications on either side. Duty left him with little time for a personal life. The only freedom he permitted himself was when he visited his mountain retreat, where both he and Annalisa could switch off from the demands of the city and rediscover the rich heritage of their flamenco gypsy roots. In the mountains he was no longer a Spanish grandee to be fawned over merely because he held a title, but Alejandro, a man to be judged alongside all others without regard to wealth or rank, and it was only in the mountains that he truly found peace.

'Alejandro!' Annalisa's voice was ever more insistent as she played to a gallery of friends. 'We need you to escort us inside!'

'I'm sure you can do that without my help,' he called back to a chorus of disappointment. His bodyguards would protect the young women, and he had laid on all the food and drink he thought necessary for a good time that wouldn't descend into chaos.

He adored his sister but would be the first to admit that he'd spoiled her. She'd been so young when their parents were killed and he'd assumed responsibility for her care. They had enjoyed the most wonderful childhood, so it was no wonder Annalisa was stricken when their parents were taken so suddenly in a tragic accident. Without a mother to confide in, she'd been lost. He'd done what he could and might have overcompensated in trying to make her feel secure again. Annalisa could be temperamental but more than made up for this with her sunny outlook on life and her ability to spread happiness. Other than where he was concerned at this moment, Alejandro conceded with some amusement as Annalisa followed him across the road.

'What do you think you're playing at, Alejandro? You promised you'd be nice to my friends.'

'And I will,' he assured her. 'My promise won't be broken, but something came up.'

'Something?' His sister, who knew him better than anyone, narrowed her eyes. 'Or someone?' she commented shrewdly. 'Just don't let this *someone* keep you too long. You'll be missed, Alejandro.'

'No, I won't,' he countered coolly as her friends watched this mini drama play out. 'You'll be too busy dancing on the table with your friends. But, be warned. I'll be back in ten minutes. And please try to remember you'll be engaged to a prince by tomorrow night, and I doubt he'll indulge you as I do when he sees your photograph splashed across the press.'

'You always were a spoilsport,' Annalisa fired back with a familiar mix of fire and love in her expression as she returned to her friends across the street.

If you mean, by calling me a spoilsport, that I love you and care for you, you're right, he mused as the door to El Gato Feroz swung wide and the maître d' rushed to greet him. He stated his wishes and the man hurried off. Dangerous seconds ticked away, during which his imagination ran riot as to what Annalisa was getting up to. Just when he thought the wait couldn't get any worse, a woman he recognised from a brief encounter years back entered the restaurant with her elderly, wealthy husband. 'Alejandro,' she purred, pausing to place a jewelled hand on his arm. 'When are you and I going to get together again?'

'Never,' he murmured discreetly as a pretty

young hostess distracted the woman's husband. 'You're married now.'

'And?'

The woman blushed guiltily as her elderly husband turned back to introduce himself to Alejandro. 'Your Excellency,' the older man exclaimed, dipping his head with respect. 'What an honour...'

'The honour is all mine,' Alejandro assured him as he returned the courtesy.

Gossip suggesting that his prowess in the bedroom was unparalleled had done him no favours at all, he reflected with amusement as the would-be siren cast a lingering glance over her shoulder when her husband ushered her away.

When the maître d' returned, his downcast expression suggested the young chef was as diligent as Alejandro had first thought her. His sympathies were with the maître d', who couldn't have looked more miserable if he'd tried. Throwing his arms wide, he exclaimed, 'I'm so sorry, Don Alejandro, but Chef Sadie is in the middle of service, and asks me to tell you that she cannot possibly be disturbed.'

'Not your fault,' he reassured the man, 'but mine for succumbing to impatience.'

Sadie. Her name was Sadie. He played the name over in his head. Well done, Sadie, he mused as he left the restaurant. This little skirmish might be over, but the battle was not lost. A smile played around his lips as he crossed the street. It pleased him to discover a woman who refused to obey his smallest whim.

Why had Don Alejandro, Duque de Alegon, asked to see her? Sadie peered out of the window as the athletic shape of one of the most famous, or should that be *infamous*, men in Spain strode across the narrow street. The Don was infamous, thanks to rumours suggesting that his expertise in business was only exceeded by his skill in bed. A quiver of awareness ran through her at the thought of all that raw, sexual energy contained in one immensely powerful individual. That was the huge difference between them right there. She had no sexual experience to speak of, and no time for it. Having seen her mother degraded by her father throughout Sadie's childhood, she was in no hurry to change the status quo. Her father had been enough to put her off men for ever, with the exception of her boss, Chef Sorollo, who was an exceptional human being, and who had always kept her safe.

It wasn't long before Sadie's thoughts strayed back to Don Alegon. No one had ever asked to speak to her personally in the middle of service, unless it was to request a special dish from the kitchen. Perhaps he'd wanted some last-minute advice on the menu for his sister's party tomorrow night. A rush of hot embarrassment swept over her, because if that were the case, she should have agreed to see him. There again, if that was what he wanted, wouldn't he deal directly with Chef Sorollo?

She glanced through the window in time to see him disappear inside Club Magia, where high society liked to congregate and check each other out. Some men with powerful physiques looked uncomfortable in a sharply cut suit, but the dark, exquisitely cut garment clung lovingly to what was undeniably a brutally masculine form.

Sadie's heart was threatening to leap out of

her chest by the time she turned back to her cooking. Why did she have to raise her head from the sauce in the first place, to see a man with the Duke's reputation staring at her? Animal instinct, she supposed; the hunter and the hunted. The feeling of being a quarry was new to her and made this brief encounter with danger all the more exciting. There was something undeniably animal about him that made her mouth dry and her body yearn for things it had never experienced, but she had more sense than to encourage a man like Don Alegon, who moved in extremely exalted circles, while this kitchen was her home.

Nothing made Sadie happier than nurturing and feeding people. Perhaps as a result of her socialite parents finding her a nuisance, she had sought out the friendship and company of their servants, and it hadn't taken long to discover the pleasure that came with making people happy by providing good food. When her father had died of one drink too many, and her mother had rejected her completely, Sadie had known exactly what she wanted to do.

* * *

The following evening Sadie and the team were making final preparations for Annalisa Alegon's engagement party when Chef Sorollo was called to the phone.

'A disaster!' the great chef wailed on his return.

Everyone in the kitchen fell silent, and everyone, Sadie was sure, was filled with the same horror-struck thought: *Not tonight!*

Even the calmest chef could lose his cool sometimes, and Chef Sorollo was not the calmest of chefs, but this outburst fell outside the range of his usual tirade and he looked genuinely shaken up. Gentle probing by Sadie revealed that a close member of his family had been taken ill. Nothing came before cooking for Chef Sorollo, apart from his immediate and extended family, which included his staff. Fortunate enough to be included in the heart of that extended family, Sadie knew she had to step up to the plate.

'Don't worry. You go. I'll take over,' she said.

'I knew I could rely on you,' her friend and mentor exclaimed with relief as he called a cab.

It was the least she could do. The great chef had been like a father to her ever since the day she'd arrived in Madrid looking for a job. Having left home and blagged her way on board a super-yacht, Sadie had soon realised that a life at sea wasn't for her, though her cooking had earned a glowing reference from the head chef in the ship's galley. When the mega-yacht had docked in Barcelona, she'd headed inland to Madrid with the dream of pursuing a career in catering, specifically at the world-renowned El Gato Feroz. Sadie had read about the famous restaurant at school and could only imagine how wonderful it would be to work alongside the famous chef. Landing the lowly position of dishwasher was like a dream come true.

'Start at the bottom and work your way up,' had been Chef Sorollo's advice. Unflinching loyalty and long hours of dedicated work in the professional kitchen was Sadie's way of paying him back.

'You've come a long way,' Chef Sorollo commented as he grabbed his coat and prepared to leave her in charge of his kitchen. 'Do you remember your first day here?' he asked, glancing outside to see if his cab had arrived.

She would never forget it. 'Vividly,' she said, remembering how, with determination etched into every fibre of her being, she had followed a member of his staff through the back door. The best part of that first day at El Gato Feroz had been meeting the world-famous chef. She could hardly believe it when he'd insisted on personally conducting her interview. Having the great man show such interest in someone who was only going to be at best a very lowly member of staff had really impressed her, and she'd never forgotten it. Dishwashing was just the start, Chef Sorollo had promised, and if she agreed to stay on late each night, he would teach her to chop vegetables. If she mastered that skill, who knew how far she could travel?

'That first day was the best day of my life,' she told him now.

'I knew this day would come,' he told her with an affectionate smile that softened the lines of worry on his face. 'I've always known I can trust you, Sadie. But don't wear yourself out tonight. There's no need to. You have a lot of support here, and Don Alegon is a good man. I've known him for years. He'll understand why our plans have been forced to change.'

Sadie wasn't quite so optimistic but said nothing to delay her friend.

'Right, team,' she announced as a cab drew up outside. 'We've got this. Let's get busy and make Chef Sorollo proud.'

'What?' Alejandro was incensed. He'd arrived early at Annalisa's party to check everything was ready, only to learn Chef Sorollo would not be in the kitchen on this most special night!

A man who never lost his temper came as close as he ever had, because this celebration was not for him, but for his sister. 'How can a head chef leave the kitchen on a night such as this?' Silverware and crystal rattled at his bellow. The hapless maître d' seemed lost for words. Not so, the woman who emerged from the kitchen. *The woman who had refused to speak to him last night.* On closer inspection she was even more beautiful, and not in a conventional way; it was the honesty shining from her eyes and the firmness of her jaw that attracted him.

'Don Alegon,' she said in the warmest of tones, 'welcome to El Gato Feroz. How nice to see you—'

'At last?' he bit out.

Ignoring his ill temper, she smiled. 'It's very good of you to drop by early to check on everything. I would do exactly the same.'

'Would you?' he challenged sharply.

'I'm sorry. I haven't introduced myself,' she said, not the least bit put off by his frosty manner. 'Chef Sadie Montgomery, at your service tonight. But, please, call me Sadie.'

'Alejandro Alegon...'

Ignoring his invitation to drop the professional barrier between them to the extent that she would call him by his first name, she held out her hand for him to shake, and said coolly, 'A pleasure to finally meet you face-to-face, Don Alegon.'

Remembering the previous night's snub, he gave her a hard stare. She smiled pleasantly. He grasped her hand briefly, but it was long enough to register a great deal about the young chef. Her hand was cool and dry, and her handshake firm and no-nonsense. It was the grip of a woman in charge. Was he wrong about the fire beneath her contained exterior? For once he doubted his initial verdict. He couldn't imagine this woman ever losing control.

'Allow me to reassure you,' she continued, 'that, in spite of Chef Sorollo's absence tonight, the menu remains unchanged, and the food will be as delicious as always at El Gato Feroz.'

'With you in charge?' He was at a loss as to how to deal with such straightforward charm and felt bound to take her to task.

'Yes,' she stated firmly, holding his stare without flinching.

Her eyes were violet, he saw now, and she used them to good effect, staring directly at him with nothing more in her expression than the desire to please, and a calm determination to soothe him now that it was glaringly obvious he wouldn't be getting the top chef he'd paid for tonight.

'I hope you're pleased with what we've

done,' she said as she led the way deeper into the restaurant. 'The team has worked really hard to make sure everything is perfect for your sister's party.'

Glancing around, he had to admit that the restaurant did look at its best. He'd requested exotic, fiery blooms to match his sister's vibrant personality, and florists had certainly worked their magic.

'We'll light the candles soon.' He stared down at the young woman at his side. 'And then you'll see how the crystal and silverware sparkles like something out of Aladdin's cave,' she added, staring into the middle distance as if picturing the scene.

So, there was a softer side to Sadie. Interesting, he thought, though she snapped out of the reverie almost immediately. As they continued the tour, she remained every inch the professional, from the crown of her chef's hat to the toes of her ugly, though sensible, shoes. It was when they accidentally brushed against each other when they moved as one to open a door that his body responded with surprising enthusiasm. He was tired of pushovers, he supposed as he took in the line of Sadie's resolute jaw.

'You have nothing to worry about, Don Alegon,' she assured him. 'We're always meticulous with planning and preparations at El Gato Feroz, and I'm confident the team has thought of everything.'

She took no praise for herself, he noticed. 'I'm not worried,' he said, and with a casual gesture he added, 'I expect the best, and I'm sure that you and your team will deliver exactly that.' Strangely, he did have confidence in Sadie.

'Thank you for putting your trust in us,' she said, seeming pleased. 'Would you like a cocktail while you wait for the guests to arrive?'

She gestured towards the famous mirrored bar with its line of deeply upholstered stools in midnight-blue velvet. 'No, thank you,' he said crisply, thinking how cold he sounded. This was the effect the city always had on him. It seemed to turn his default setting to tense, and when his sister was added to the mix, his desire for excellence was off the scale.

'Can't I tempt you with a glass of champagne?'

She could tempt him with many things, he thought as she stared into his eyes, but not champagne. He wanted a clear head tonight. His doubts on the wisdom of Annalisa's choice of husband remained, and he needed to keep a watchful eye on the Prince and his friends. They might have grand titles, but a thorough investigation by his security team had proved they didn't have the money to fund their extravagant lifestyles, and when his sister was in one of her reckless moods, she might not see trouble looming on the horizon as he did.

'Champagne? No, thank you,' he told Sadie.

'Beer, then?' she suggested with the hint of a mocking light in her eyes.

She was not afraid to tease and test him, which was another point in her favour. 'A beer would be good. But only if you join me.'

Her polite smile didn't falter as she told him, 'I never drink on duty.'

They stared at each other with renewed interest until she said, 'I believe your sister's arriving, so I'll have one of the waiters bring you your beer.'

Before he could say another word, she had gone. Once again, eluding him, he thought, grinding his jaw. Before he had chance to dwell on this, the fleet of stretch limos he'd ordered to accommodate Annalisa and her friends drew up outside the restaurant. He'd be too busy for the rest of the evening to talk to Sadie, but she'd thrown down a gauntlet he wouldn't forget.

CHAPTER TWO

IT WOULD BE a late night before she climbed into bed in the tiny attic above the restaurant, but there was nothing she wouldn't do for Chef Sorollo, and Sadie was enjoying every moment of being in charge of the kitchen. It was the first time she had been put to the test, and she was determined to shine for her mentor.

'Service!' she called out for the umpteenth time, remembering back to when the great man had asked her if she had anywhere to live. From the off Chef Sorollo had shown piercing intuition, understanding so much without her having to say a single word. 'I have a room,' he'd said. 'It's not much, but it's somewhere to lay your head.'

Sadie smiled to think she'd lived there ever since. The simple bedsit with its view over the rooftops of Madrid was spotlessly clean and extremely comfortable, and, best of all, it was quiet. There was no shouting, no china crashing to the floor and no violence. There was just the hum of purposeful activity in the restaurant kitchen far below. Some might have thought it a comedown after the brash opulence of her parents' home, but Sadie had always felt like a clumsy intruder in the huge, echoing mansion, with its screening room, swim-up bar, and regular shouting matches.

'Everyone loves it, Sadie,' one of the waiters exclaimed as he swept past her as if on oiled wheels. 'Your party's a huge success.'

'Our party,' she called after him, smiling.

With a little gentle prompting by Chef Sorollo, her story had come out. The great man had insisted on taking charge of her education, sending her to night school, where she'd formally trained to be a chef. When she was qualified, he'd taken her under his wing and had completed her training, saying that a loyal and loving family stayed close and looked after each other. That was why work consumed her now, and why there had never been a more important night for Sadie—because this was her way of thanking a man who had turned out to be her saviour.

Excellence was paramount tonight. With so many celebrated guests present, the papers would report Annalisa Alegon's party, and there would be photographs of everyone present. A shiver ran down her spine at the thought of one guest in particular. She'd had chance to read up on Don Alejandro de Alegon and had learned something of his colourful history. He was descended from a long line of aristocrats on his father's side, while his late mother had been a Spanish gypsy princess. Both his parents had been killed in a tragic accident, leaving Alejandro to raise his younger sister. Everyone thought it a great honour that he'd chosen El Gato Feroz as the venue for his sister's engagement party. Sadie guessed he made all the choices; even on the briefest sighting, he'd struck her as that type of man. He played out his life on the world stage while she was content in the kitchen, and she would never belong in his world any more than she had belonged in her parents' world. Bottom line: the Don commanded while she was happy to serve.

Serve him?

Certainly not! Sadie concluded with a short laugh as she served up a fresh batch of delicious entrées. The thought that there was no buffer between Sadie and Don Alegon in the comforting form of Chef Sorollo might make her tense, but she would allow nothing to get in the way of making tonight the success her mentor and his team deserved. It would be business as usual tonight at El Gato Feroz.

For the rest of the night he was aware of Sadie somewhere close by, and he looked for her constantly. No other woman had ever affected him this way, and he couldn't explain the feeling. It took his sister linking arms with him to return his attention to where it should have been all along.

'I can't thank you enough for tonight,' Annalisa said as she snuggled into his side. 'It's more than I deserve—'

'A lot more,' he agreed dryly.

They laughed together. Annalisa was the one

person in the world who could shake him out of his city tension. There were so many plates to keep spinning he could barely spare her a moment when he was in Madrid, but Annalisa had always gone where angels feared to tread, and tonight was a special occasion.

'Are you happy? Are you sure about the Prince?' he asked with concern as his glance swept over the man in question and his party, who were doing their best to drain the last bottle of wine in the cellar of El Gato Feroz.

'I know I love you,' his sister told him fervently as she stared up into his eyes. 'You do know that, don't you, Alejandro? You're so stern, I wonder sometimes if you realise how much I appreciate all you do for me. I just hope the day will come when I can do something for you.'

'Behave yourself,' he said mock sternly. 'That's what I want you to do. And don't worry about me.'

'But I do worry about you,' Annalisa insisted. 'You should be thinking about your life going forward, not mine. What would it take to make you happy, Alejandro?'

'Whatever it takes for you to have a good life,' he said, glancing with concern at Annalisa's husband-to-be, who seemed more interested in talking to the pretty woman at his side than looking after his sister. 'You will tell me if anything goes wrong, won't you?'

'I know you're always there for me,' she said. 'But I don't want to talk about me, I want to talk about you. It's time you did something for yourself, instead of always for other people. You deserve happiness too.'

'Nobody *deserves* anything,' he stated firmly. 'You just concentrate on your upcoming new life as a princess.' As he said this, he wondered how much of Annalisa's latest romance was based on the idea of becoming a princess, rather than the reality of marrying such a weak man. His sister wasn't a fool, but she was a dreamer. It wasn't up to him to live Annalisa's life for her, he reminded himself, though living up to that wasn't easy. 'Happiness is fleeting,' he warned as he held her gaze. 'Grab it while you can.'

'That's a lesson for you too,' his sister told him. 'I know you're thinking about our parents when you say things like this, and I also know they'd want you to be happy. Grab some happiness while you can, Alejandro, and hug it tight.'

He smiled. 'You're a lovely young woman and I'm very proud of you. You know that, don't you?'

'If I don't,' his sister assured him with one of her sideways looks, 'I'm sure I can rely on you to tell me.'

They laughed together, and for a few moments everything was simple and warm, as it had always been before the Prince came on the scene. 'Just make sure you tell me if the Prince lets you down,' he said, turning serious.

'You'll be the first to know—your cast-iron security team will make sure of it,' Annalisa added with a cheeky glance as she turned away to her friends.

He watched the young women in their huddle at the table, wondering what they were discussing so avidly. He soon found out.

'We want the chef to step out so we can thank her for the most marvellous evening,' Annalisa came to tell him.

'Annalisa!' he exclaimed as she bolted away. Too late. She'd already attracted the attention of the maître d'.

A few minutes later, his sister returned with a slightly pinker version of Sadie, who emerged from the kitchen to a storm of applause. In spite of Chef Sorello's absence, the food had been absolutely delicious and everything had gone without a hitch. He surprised himself by leading the applause, and even offering a personal vote of thanks. When their eyes met, Sadie held his stare with that same mix of professional cool and not quite hidden glint of something more. It was a combination that made his senses roar.

It was the early hours before the guests began to leave. As the restaurant emptied, he stepped outside to find a hint of dawn tinting the night sky lavender. It was a particular light that reminded him of daybreak in the mountains he loved, because it was there, in the wild, dramatic land of his mother's people, where he felt most at ease. His mother and father's very different personalities would always war inside him, he supposed. Striving to be the best of both of them was his life's work. His mother had bequeathed vision and passion, while his father had instilled in him a stern sense of responsibility that insisted his life in the city must always take precedence, because it was here that he cared for his sister and ran a business upon which countless families depended for their livelihood. This thought was only underlined when he noticed Annalisa's fiancé, the Prince, ignoring the wait staff as he strode out of the restaurant, surrounded by his cronies.

'Where is he going?' he asked Annalisa as she stared after the Prince with concern.

'To a club, I think…to celebrate our engagement,' she added quickly when he stared at her, frowning.

'The very least the staff deserve after such a marvellous evening is a word of thanks. And shouldn't you have a lift home? Don't worry, I'll take you,' he said, seeing Annalisa's crestfallen expression. Why such a generous-hearted woman should attract such selfish men was utterly beyond him.

He made up for the Prince's oversight by

giving the staff the recognition they deserved, and he enjoyed talking to each of them in turn to thank them personally for making the evening so special for his sister. His only irritation was that when it came to showing his appreciation to the woman who'd saved the night, Sadie was nowhere to be found.

Resting back on her narrow bed in the attic room above the restaurant, Sadie sighed with relief and contentment…marred with just a little bit of racing heartbeat, thanks to a pair of dangerous dark eyes that kept flashing back and forth inside her mind. At least she could report to Chef Sorollo that everything had gone well. And now that she was back in her safe place, she was confident she would never need anything more than this.

Except relief from images of the Duque de Alegon, Sadie concluded with an impatient huff as she punched her pillows into submission. Turning over repeatedly also failed to banish the all too vivid picture of Alejandro de Alegon. It was ridiculous. She'd probably never see him again. Which would be far better for all concerned, Sadie concluded. He stirred such turbulent feelings inside her, and she'd learned as a small child that passion was a destructive force that led to nowhere but anger and violence. Witnessing her parents' unhappy relationship had more than proved that.

Closing her eyes, she turned her thoughts determinedly to what had been an astonishing evening. What a setting! What a night! The team had really proved their worth. And then there were the looks she'd shared with Don Alegon…she'd remember those for ever.

So much for blotting him out of her mind!

Alejandro…

She murmured his name out loud, for the pleasure of tasting it on her tongue. Imagining his firm lips on hers, and his lean, bronzed hands leading her towards the type of pleasure she couldn't even imagine, was inevitable.

And that's enough! she told herself firmly. However wonderful the evening had been, she would wake up in a few hours, shower and change, ready to prepare lunch.

Service in the restaurant at lunchtime the next day didn't go as smoothly as Sadie had anticipated. It seemed incredible that, yet again, a crisis had stopped everyone in their tracks.

'Oh, my God, no!' Sadie exclaimed, incapable of hiding her feelings when she heard the news. Gripping the stainless-steel countertop to steady herself, she tried to take in the newsflash on a colleague's phone. Complete with lurid pictures, it showed a car crash, and the text underneath read that Alejandro, the Duque de Alegon, and his sister, Annalisa, had been innocent victims of a pile-up on their way home from a party last night at El Gato Feroz.

Seeing Annalisa so happy only hours before, and Alejandro so vital and strong, she hardly dared to ask the question. 'Are they badly hurt?'

One of her fellow chefs was quick to reassure her. 'They were relatively unscathed, it says in a later bulletin,' he explained, showing her the screen on his phone. 'It's a miracle, some are saying, especially as Don Alegon risked his life, saving his sister from the smoke-filled car. They're keeping them in hospital as a precautionary measure only, it says here.'

'His sister would be dead if the Duke hadn't been such a hero,' a waiter added. 'Apparently, he barely had time to free her before the car exploded.'

'Sadie, are you okay?' a colleague asked with concern. 'Shall I get you a drink of water?'

'It's fortunate the Duke drank water last night, unlike the Prince and his friends,' one of the waitresses chipped in. 'Don Alegon drank one beer, and then he was on water for the rest of the night.'

'It says so here in the report,' Sadie confirmed as she read the screen over her fellow chef's shoulder. 'The police have confirmed that Don Alegon had not been drinking to excess and was in no way responsible for the crash.'

'Look, here's a picture of the party,' one of Sadie's colleagues exclaimed excitedly, holding up her phone. 'There's a picture of you,

Sadie, when you came out of the kitchen and everyone applauded. What great publicity for the restaurant. Chef Sorollo will be thrilled.'

'Yes,' Sadie murmured as the phone was pushed under her nose. She blushed to see Alejandro's black gaze fixed on her face. 'Maybe we could send him some food from the kitchen,' she murmured distractedly, hoping no one else had noticed Don Alegon devouring her with his eyes.

When her colleagues chorused, 'What a good idea,' she progressed the thought. 'Some delicacies,' Sadie mused out loud, already working out a menu in her head. 'Something to tempt the invalid.' A voice in her head suggested Don Alegon would not be a typical invalid but would rail against his enforced confinement.

However bad a mood he was in, he'd saved his sister, and that was good enough for Sadie. She would prepare a feast that even Alejandro at his angriest would find impossible to resist.

'What the hell is this?' Lifting the red-and-white gingham cloth that had been so carefully arranged over the wicker basket, Alejandro lost no time in firing the contents into the bin.

'You ungrateful brute!' his sister railed at him, eyes blazing with fury. 'How could you?'

'Whoever sent this must think I'm not capable of ordering in!'

'Chef Sadie sent it,' Annalisa fired back. 'It was a very kind thought. You should be ashamed of yourself,' his sister finished with an angry gesture worthy of any great actress.

Sadie had sent this? He scanned the delicacies in the bin, regretting now that he'd been so hasty. His customary good manners had utterly deserted him, thanks to this enforced stay in hospital. It didn't help his temper one bit—having imagined himself invincible—that Annalisa had been discharged from hospital before him.

'If you weren't my brother and you hadn't saved my life, I'd be ashamed of you,' Annalisa now assured him. 'I *am* ashamed of you. How dare you throw this kindness back in Sadie's face? Who else would send you food?' Shoving a stiff white card under his nose, she commanded, 'Read this. She's signed it and so has every member of staff at El Gato Feroz. I hope it makes you feel as bad as you should, you monster.'

'Back in bed!' The sharp voice from the doorway startled them both. It was the ward sister making her rounds. 'You breathed in a lot of smoke, Don Alegon,' she told him, 'and what you need now is rest.'

'What I need now is to get out of here,' he argued tensely. 'And what about my sister? She was in the accident too. Shouldn't she be resting?'

'I managed to keep my head out of the window,' Annalisa piped up, 'so I was breathing fresh air. Braving the smoke to save me forced you to breathe in a lot of smoke, so do as the ward sister says and get back into bed.'

'Am I a caged beast now?' he grumbled, only to be greeted by peals of laughter from both women.

'You're an ungrateful beast,' Annalisa confirmed, and as the ward sister left them to continue her rounds she began to forage in the bin. 'What if *I* had wanted to eat some of this?'

Fortunately most of it was boxed and, having

salvaged a container of freshly baked *macar-
rones*, Annalisa was cramming her favourites
into her mouth before offering the rest to him.
He refused, of course.

'You don't deserve anyone to be kind to
you,' she flashed. 'The least you can do is
write a thank-you note to Sadie for preparing
all this lovely food.'

He growled but found he couldn't summon
up any anger. Quite a different emotion was
plaguing him at the thought of Sadie going to
all this trouble, and it was one that ensured
that as soon as he was discharged, he would
thank Sadie in person.

'You're still my responsibility,' he informed
Annalisa, 'and you'll do as I say.'

'Oh?' she queried. 'Am I not in the charge
of my soon-to-be husband?'

'That puny excuse for a man,' he bit out,
no longer able to hide his true feelings for
his sister's fiancé in his present state of mind.
Annalisa wouldn't even have been in the car
accident if her fiancé had done what he was
supposed to have done and taken care of her,
escorting her home. 'Tell me you sent him

packing?' Hope rose inside him when his sister hesitated before answering.

'Take a note, Don Alejandro,' Annalisa retorted, smashing his hopes into the ground. 'I'm all grown up, and I'll make my own decisions without consulting you first.'

'Is it over?' he pressed.

'None of your business. And you can stay in bed,' she added sharply. 'I won't have you towering over me and attempting to bend me to your will.'

As if, he thought, trying not to smile. 'Where are you going now?' he demanded as Annalisa made for the door.

'To El Gato Feroz,' she fired back. 'One of us has to thank Chef Sadie, if only to prove that not all the Alegons are arrogant, ungrateful brutes.'

'Come back here!'

'No,' she flashed. 'If you can't do anything to help yourself, then it's up to me to do something to help you.' Leaving him with that disturbing thought, his sister stormed out.

The spartan hospital room was unbearably quiet when Annalisa left. Was she right? Was

Annalisa ready to take charge of her life, and was he guilty of interfering? Caring for his sister had been such an overwhelming force inside him for so long, he didn't know how to let it go. The thought that Annalisa might need space from him had never occurred to him before, and would take some getting used to.

Where better to do that than in the mountains he loved, where his lungs would soon heal? He would discharge himself. The accident had put life in perspective, proving how fragile it was, and allowing him to see that he had never examined his grief of losing his parents. There hadn't been chance with the weight of responsibility eating up every minute of every day. Annalisa and the business had always taken priority over personal concerns, but he couldn't carry out his duties effectively with such an unreasonably short fuse. The time had come to heal his soul as well as his body.

CHAPTER THREE

Sadie exclaimed with happy surprise when Annalisa Alegon turned up at the restaurant. 'Señorita de Alegon! How lovely to see you again, and what a relief to see you looking so well!'

Annalisa looked gorgeous in a simple, flower-patterned summer dress that showed off her bronzed limbs to best advantage. She had teamed the sky-blue confection with delicate strappy sandals, huge sunglasses, and a beribboned straw hat with a wide brim on top of her flowing black hair.

'And your brother?' Sadie held her breath as she waited for the answer.

'First off, I am, and always will be, Annalisa to you,' Annalisa insisted as she enveloped Sadie in a hug. 'As for my brother? Predictably, he's grouchy. Confinement doesn't suit him.' She shrugged. 'Our heritage, I suppose. But let's not talk about him. I'm here to thank you for last night. It was such a wonderful occasion. And, of course, for the delicious treats you sent to the hospital.'

At the mention of the word hospital, Sadie paled. 'Was your brother able to enjoy the food I sent over?'

Annalisa slanted an amused look at Sadie. 'He was most appreciative.'

Her face remained carefully expressionless, leaving Sadie free to guess the rest. 'All I care about is that you're both safe. It was such a shock to hear about the accident.'

'I'd have been burnt to a crisp without Alejandro,' Annalisa stated bluntly. 'He's the best of men, you know.'

'I'm sure he is,' Sadie agreed politely.

'Are *you* all right?' she asked suddenly, with concern, keen to divert attention away from how she felt about Alejandro.

'A little delayed shock, I think,' Annalisa admitted with a dismissive shrug. 'Inevitable, I suppose. An accident like that really shakes you up and proves how vulnerable we all are.

I keep thinking, what would I do without Alejandro?'

Sadie smiled. 'I saw how close you are.' It was on the tip of her tongue to ask if Annalisa's fiancé had taken care of her too, but instinct kept her quiet. She hadn't liked the Prince, or his friends. 'So, your brother's to remain in hospital?' she asked instead.

'And as stubborn as ever,' Annalisa confirmed. 'Though knowing Alejandro, I doubt they'll be able to keep him there for long.'

'Shouldn't he give himself chance to recover? I heard he inhaled a lot of smoke.'

'True, but Alejandro taking things slowly is never going to happen. And he has his own ideas when it comes to convalescing. Chopping logs, swimming in freezing cold lakes and riding flat out on the plateau above the mountains suits him better than a hospital bed. Quite literally anything that takes him away from the city for a while. You wouldn't know him when he visits our mother's people. He's a different man. They regard him as a king, but Alejandro assures me that it's only when he's in the mountains that he's pared down to the better man beneath all the hype and celebrity that status brings him in Madrid.'

Fascinated, Sadie was desperate to learn more. 'Can I offer you a coffee, or perhaps a cold drink?'

'I'd love a coffee, if you've got time,' Annalisa agreed.

Sadie would make time, not just to learn more about a man who had affected her so profoundly, but because Annalisa looked a little lost, as if she needed a friend to confide in as much as Sadie. 'Of course I've got time,' she confirmed warmly as she indicated an empty table where they could sit.

Annalisa's opening gambit couldn't have surprised Sadie more. 'I don't want to cause any trouble,' she said as they sat down.

'Drinking coffee?' Sadie remarked lightly, wondering what was coming next. 'I don't think there's too much risk in that. If there's anything at all I can help you with…' she added as Annalisa played with her coffee spoon.

'There is something you could help me with,' Annalisa blurted. 'I'm worried about my brother. He's far more important to me than anyone else.'

'You're worried about Don Alegon?'

'Alejandro,' Annalisa prompted.

'Well, Alejandro seems tough enough to withstand whatever life throws at him.' Unless his injuries were worse than the press had reported, Sadie thought with a stab of alarm. 'His condition hasn't deteriorated, has it?'

'No,' Annalisa exclaimed quickly, to reassure them both, Sadie thought.

'His voice is still scratchy, and, of course, he could do with some fuss, as well as someone he'll actually listen to when they tell him to slow down. It's just a pity I can't get up to the mountains at the moment, because I have other things to sort out.'

'If there's anything I can do—'

'With my brother heading to Sierra Nevada—and I know he will once he leaves hospital—he'll need someone to care for him—to make sure he eats his food—that sort of thing—someone he'll listen to when they tell him not to overdo the exercise...'

Annalisa was being a little optimistic, Sadie

thought, and there was something suspiciously like a question in her eyes. 'Oh, no, I can't,' Sadie said quickly.

'Even slight damage to the lungs can be quite serious,' Annalisa added, adopting a mournful look. 'I really think he needs someone to supervise his recovery.'

'I can imagine how that would go down,' Sadie commented dryly.

'But if anyone could do it, you could,' Annalisa insisted, brightening as she continued to work on convincing Sadie.

'You're asking me to go there uninvited?'

'I'd explain to my brother first,' Annalisa assured her with eyes that were wide and appealing.

'So, let me get this straight. You're asking me to go to the Sierra Nevada mountains to look after your brother who doesn't know I'm coming?'

'Until I tell him,' Annalisa exclaimed.

'And you would tell him?'

'Of course—and you'll love it there,' she added enthusiastically. 'It might not be Madrid, but the mountains are very beautiful, and

I've never seen my brother's face light up as it does when he looks at you.'

'What?'

'Obviously, your food is delicious,' Annalisa said, backtracking fast. 'But I know he likes you too. And with food being the way to a man's heart...'

The persuasive tactics continued, as Annalisa remained stubbornly oblivious to Sadie's growing doubts as to the wisdom of her plan.

Convinced she was being set up, Sadie finally interrupted. 'Surely a man like Alejandro can employ any chef in the world?'

'He loves your food best,' Annalisa countered quickly. 'And I'm sure he'd recover faster if you're on hand.'

On hand? Sadie queried silently. To do what? More than cooking? Annalisa might be a novice matchmaker, but she had made a great case, and Sadie was actually severely tempted to go to the mountains to discover if Alejandro really was a different man when he was there. Sensibly, she resisted the temptation and made her refusal as gentle as she could. 'I don't think I'm the right person for the job, but I might be able to find a private chef who I'm sure would be only too pleased to cook for your brother.'

'He wants you—' Annalisa blushed furiously. 'I mean, he wants you to cook for him. It's your food he likes. Please say you'll do it. I don't have time to interview any other applicants, and I'm afraid for his health.'

'His scratchy voice?' Sadie remarked dryly.

'Busted,' Annalisa conceded with a theatrical huff. Sitting back, she cocked her chin to share an amused look with Sadie. 'But, honestly, he does need you, and as his sister I have a duty to tell you that. Come on, Sadie—what do you have to lose? If you hate him, you can take a look at the antiquated kitchen. You'd be doing both of us a favour if you could offer suggestions on its renovation.'

'Doesn't he have a housekeeper to do that?'

'Yes, of course,' Annalisa confirmed, 'but it's not her job to redesign the kitchen, and you have so much more experience...'

'Please,' she added after both women had been silent for a while. 'Alejandro does so much for everyone, and I want to do something for him.'

'I'm not sure he likes me as much as you think he does. We've only met once, though I'm very pleased to hear that he likes my cooking. But if he goes to the mountains for solitude, and to be himself, as you have explained, I can't imagine he'll want to see me.'

'But you can handle him. You won't let him boss you around. And, of course, you'll make him eat all that delicious food you prepare.'

'Spoon-feed him?' Sadie suggested, tongue-in-cheek.

'You can try,' Annalisa agreed with a laugh. 'Please…for me,' she repeated as Sadie drained her coffee. 'You've nothing to worry about. He prefers horses to people, and keeps his best mounts at his mountain retreat, so you'll probably hardly ever see him.'

Sadie pushed her cup and saucer to one side, giving them a few moments of thinking space. 'I'd really love to help,' she admitted, staring Annalisa in the eyes, 'but it's impossible for me to leave the restaurant.'

'Who says you can't?' Chef Sorollo demanded as he walked past.

'You're back,' Sadie exclaimed with relief, springing up. 'Is everything all right at home?'

'Yes, thank you. False alarm. I was more concerned to hear about the car crash,' he added, and, turning to Annalisa, he took both her hands in his. 'How are you, Señorita Alegon, and how is your brother?'

Explanations and expressions of relief were exchanged, before Chef Sorollo turned back to Sadie. 'Did I just overhear you saying that you can't take any time off work? I'm back, as you can see,' he declared expansively, tapping his chest with both hands, 'and no one deserves a break more than you. You're no good to me exhausted, Sadie.'

'Exactly what I was thinking,' Annalisa exclaimed, brightening now that she had an ally and success within her grasp. 'I've just explained to Sadie that if she could possibly go and cook for my brother for a little while, it would aid his recovery—'

'Good thinking,' Chef Sorollo cut in, and, carrying the baton forward, he added, 'Your brother did ask me if I could visit his mountain retreat at some point, to advise on the renovation of the kitchen. Why, Sadie, that's the perfect job for you!'

Set-up! sounded loud in Sadie's ears, but what could she do about it, when two of the nicest people she knew had decided to range their forces against her?

'The mountain air will do you good,' Chef Sorollo declared. 'It will be so refreshing, and, apart from advising on the kitchen, you can source some new recipes for El Gato Feroz. Perfect!' he enthused. 'The cuisine in the mountain villages is said to be second to none. Good. I'm glad that's settled,' he added before Sadie had chance to say a word.

'So, you'll do it?' Annalisa asked, barely able to contain her excitement as she leaned across the table.

The alternative was to refuse to do something for Chef Sorollo, who had done so much for Sadie. 'Yes,' Sadie confirmed, biting down on everything else she'd like to say, but couldn't when it involved her mentor. She might have felt marginally more upbeat about the forthcoming trip if she hadn't seen the glint of amusement in the great chef's eyes.

The sun was blazing down in the village square when Sadie finally arrived in the mountains after a long and tiring journey. She was somewhere close to Alejandro's mountain retreat, but wasn't sure of the precise details, as Annalisa had promised someone would meet her. Well, that someone hadn't turned up. She'd been waiting for the promised lift for about an hour while village life bustled on around her. At least the surroundings were magnificent. Shading her eyes, she stared up at the majestic snow-capped peaks of the Sierra Nevada, noticing that the paths leading up were steep and rocky, and utterly uninviting in the heat of the sun.

Seeing an elderly lady looking at Sadie as if she would like to help, Sadie asked, 'El Castillo Fuego?'

'*Es menos de tres millas—*'

'I'm sorry?'

The elderly woman pointed out a tree-lined track.

'It's less than three miles to the castle,' she explained in heavily accented English. 'Once you get past the smooth lower slopes the trail is a bit tricky, but you should arrive before it gets too hot for walking if you leave now,' she added helpfully.

'So, there's no transport going up there?' Sadie asked, hope dwindling as she stared apprehensively at the long and winding path.

'There is only walking, or the helicopter used by El Duque.' This was said with a glow of admiration in the old lady's voice.

'Excellent,' Sadie said, trying not to sound too dejected.

'There are some mule trains…'

Sadie brightened.

'But not today.'

'Well, thank you very much for the information.' She held back on her thoughts of El Duque soaring effortlessly up the mountain to his secluded retreat, leaving her to slog up to his remote castle on foot.

'You can't miss El Castillo Fuego,' the old lady promised as Sadie adjusted a backpack that seemed to have doubled in weight at the prospect of the climb ahead. 'It dominates the landscape for miles around.'

'I can't wait to see it.' Determined she wouldn't be beaten, she added brightly, 'And thank you again for the help.'

Well, at least she had a plan now. Arrive. Feed the invalid. Assess the kitchen. Leave.

Sadie remained upbeat for approximately five hundred yards, after which it became clear that working in a kitchen had done nothing to prepare her for the outdoor life. If this was 'smooth' walking, she dreaded to think what the top part of the track would be like.

This was what he needed, Alejandro concluded as his stallion picked a safe route down the path. Freedom, fresh air, with just the wind in his face and the sound of the nearby waterfall cascading down the cliff, punctuated by the intermittent cry of an eagle.

And a cry for help?

In English?

In a voice that sounded uncannily like Chef Sadie's?

Instantly, he saw his sister's hand in this. Not

satisfied with mollycoddling him after the accident, Annalisa had sent what she perceived to be an angel of mercy to cook for him. And now the angel needed assistance.

Urging his horse around a rocky outcrop faster than safety allowed, he found himself confronted by the most astonishing scene.

His stallion snorted its disapproval as he brought it skidding to a halt. Assessing the situation at a glance, he saw that Sadie was in no real danger, but she was lucky he'd ridden by. Poorly prepared for the mountains, she'd been let down by her footwear on the rocky trail. She'd slipped on the shale, and the straps of her backpack had become entangled in a tree. At the angle she was caught, she had no chance of freeing herself, but her feet were on the ground, so she was in no danger of falling any further down the slope.

'What the hell are you doing here?' he demanded.

'Hanging around?'

He wasn't amused. 'For how long?'

'Ten minutes or so. Does it matter?'

'It would if I hadn't ridden by.'

Her scowl made him laugh.

'You think this is funny?' she flashed with a frown.

What might have maddened him in the city—Sadie's naivety; the risk she'd taken to walk up a track she didn't know—irritated him, but relief that he had found her overcame everything...not that he wouldn't make her suffer for a while.

'Are you just going to sit there?' she demanded.

'Don't tempt me.'

Her answer was a snort of disgust.

The slope of the land meant they were at eye level, and if the straps on her backpack gave way, the worst that could happen was that she would roll a couple of yards down the hill. 'I'm not sure I've got time for this,' he said as he wheeled his horse around. 'Thor is hungry and impatient to get home. If he should bolt—'

'Bolt?' she scoffed. 'Weren't you born in the saddle?'

'In a caravan, actually.'

She shrugged. 'If you've finished staring, I'd appreciate a hand getting down.'

'You haven't told me why you're here,' he said, and with considerable restraint, in his opinion.

'I'm supposed to be checking out your kitchens, as requested by Chef Sorollo, so I can advise on a refurbishment,' she informed him tetchily, 'but I can hardly do that while I'm swinging from a tree.'

'Clearly.' His lips pressed down as he frowned. 'I did ask Chef Sorollo for advice.'

'And he decided to send me. Now can you please get me down?'

He was in no hurry. The view was good from here. Sadie's hair was a rich, vibrant red-gold, and he'd never seen it cascading free before. It fell to her waist in such glorious abandon, he could imagine it would look that way after they made love.

'And Annalisa said you needed someone to take care of you,' she added. 'Apparently, there was some damage to your voice? Are you okay?' she asked with sudden concern.

'I appear to be.'

She appeared relieved, and then she bridled.

'No hurry,' she said sarcastically. 'I'm happy to hang around here all day.'

'In that case—'

'Don't you dare,' she warned as he turned his horse.

'You'll keep.'

'What's that supposed to mean?' she yelled after him.

He rode a short distance before coming back. 'Thank goodness,' she exclaimed with relief. 'You *are* going to get me down?' she asked with sudden doubt ringing in her voice.

He shrugged. 'Both Thor and I need feeding.'

She said something rude under her breath while he positioned his stallion beneath her. Unsheathing his knife, he sliced through the straps of her backpack, and as she fell, he caught her. Lifting her onto the saddle in front of him, he locked an arm around her waist. 'You are the most annoying woman I have ever met. Either you won't see me, or I can't get away from you. And only the fact that I refuse to leave you to plague the poor mountain lions when they come to eat you encourages me to take you with me. We'll discuss your stupidity in the morning,' he added over Sadie's spluttering reply.

'*My* stupidity?' she exclaimed with affront.

'Wandering around a mountain you're unfamiliar with, in unsuitable clothing? What else would you call it?'

'I was told I'd be met when I arrived,' she countered hotly.

'Well, no one told me,' he assured her, 'or I would have instructed you not to come.'

'*Instructed* me?' she exclaimed with outrage.

So, there was fire beneath that cool exterior. It seemed the mountains had changed them both.

Urging his stallion forward when they hit a flatter piece of ground, he said, 'I hope you can ride.'

'I've been riding since I was a child,' she told him. 'So, you're quite safe to let me go.'

'I'll be the judge of that. My stallion's suffered enough delay for one day, and the last thing I need is you falling off.'

As she huffed her displeasure, he registered how good it felt to have Sadie pressed up hard against him. She was more toned than he had expected, though soft in all the right places. Strong, yet vulnerable, he thought, and, though he had briefly resented the fact that his precious solitude had been interrupted, he found himself looking forward to the next few days. 'Hold on,' he said as he pushed Thor into a gallop when they reached some flat ground.

'Do you think I'm going to drop off like a pile of old rubbish?'

'I wouldn't describe you quite like that,' he said dryly as Sadie turned to flash him an angry glance.

'How would you describe me?' she asked after a few moments when she had settled into the rhythm of his horse.

He smiled and said nothing. That was one question he had no intention of answering just yet.

CHAPTER FOUR

ALEJANDRO FELT INCREDIBLE as they rode together in perfect harmony. Muscular, hard, fit and strong, he was so confident and commanding on horseback. As Annalisa had predicted, he was very different in the mountains. There was even the suggestion of a sense of humour, which only added to his blistering appeal. Hot as hell in banged-up jeans and a tightly fitting T-shirt, faded through years of use, and smelling of sunshine and warm, clean man, he was no longer the stern aristocrat, the stylish Don, but a rugged man of the mountains with wild hair and dangerous eyes. He was also relaxed enough to tease, which felt like the prelude to something else…something far more alarming, and yet exciting. It wasn't every day she got to ride a formidable stallion with a man as competent on horseback as Alejandro.

Would he be as good at everything else?

Almost certainly, Sadie decided, smiling at the thought of spending time with him.

'You sit well on a horse,' he said, distracting her from these dangerous thoughts.

She had to take several deep, steadying breaths, straighten up and put a few inches between them before she could even think straight enough to answer this observation. 'I spent a lot of time in the stables as a child,' she admitted. When it had been a case of doing anything to put distance between Sadie and her warring parents. 'Horses were always the best company, I found.' Just as well, since friends weren't allowed in the house. Her mother would always say there were too many antiques for them to damage.

'I think the owner of the nearby stables must have got fed up, seeing me peering longingly through his fence, and so he taught me to ride. I haven't had much opportunity to ride a horse since then, because I've been working, but this is fabulous and I'm really enjoying it.'

Sadie's attempt to keep her voice level and matter-of-fact failed, but what the hell? she thought. She was enjoying herself, and wasn't afraid to admit it. After the shock of Alejandro's accident, and then the fright of wondering if anyone would find her on the mountain, this was just amazing.

'I keep horses here, but don't ever ride out on your own,' Alejandro warned in a stern tone that sent a quiver of awareness streaking through her. 'You don't know the trail.'

But she'd like to. She'd like to know a lot of things. But then, to her surprise, he started chatting easily. Alejandro wanted to know about Sadie, and she didn't get the chance to ask him all the things she would have liked to, about his home in the mountains, and his heritage, and the magic that drew him here time after time.

He asked about her schooling, which she'd loved, and how she'd got into catering as a career. 'You're quite a determined person,' he commented when she had finished detailing her CV.

'I like to get things done,' she admitted.

'You nearly did for yourself this time.'

'It was unfortunate,' she agreed, 'but lucky that you came along.'

As Alejandro grunted disapprovingly, she vowed to question him when she got the chance. And then they rounded the final stretch of the trail, and his grand mountain residence loomed in front of them.

Having imagined something magnificent, but fairly conventional—if any castle could be called conventional—she was astounded to see that Alejandro's mountain home was colossal and built into a cliff.

'It was originally an old monastery,' he explained.

She could see that now, and how suitable for a man who sought peace and solitude away from the demands of the city. But there was another side to Alejandro she'd heard about, and that was the Gypsy King, and it was this man she was desperate to see. She'd got a hint of him on the trail: powerful, fierce, awe-inspiring.

What would it be like to have a gypsy king for a lover?

And why was she even thinking like that? Hardly a duchess, she was certainly not gypsy queen material. Cook, sleep, wash and cook again was how she lived, and so far it had suited her.

Really?

Yes, Sadie told her inner voice firmly as she stared again at the awe-inspiring monastery perched on the edge of what appeared to be a sheer granite cliff. The eyrie for the eagle, she thought, wondering what lay inside.

They rode through the impressive entrance and into a stone courtyard large enough to house a couple of football pitches. Springing down from his stallion, Alejandro reached up to help her down. The sure touch of his hands on her arms sent bolts of electricity shooting through her, and she blushed as they stared properly into each other's face for the first time since the rescue. Alejandro's expression was unreadable, but it carried a powerful charge. It didn't help that he was the most beautiful man she had ever seen, with his thickly lashed eyes beneath sweeping ebony brows, and those chiselled cheekbones and that sensuous mouth that would have sent Michelangelo into a creative frenzy.

Enough! She shouldn't be thinking about his eyes. She was here to work, and maybe do a little bit of coddling, though Alejandro hardly looked in need of any fuss. 'This woman is exhausted,' he explained to her surprise, addressing an older woman who had emerged from one of the doors leading into the building.

So, he was concerned for her welfare. In fairness, she'd probably given him quite a shock. The mountain was no place for novice hikers, which was a lesson she'd learned and would remember in future.

'Please escort Señorita Sadie to one of the guest rooms, and make sure she has something to eat, as well as a warm bath.'

'I'm quite capable of walking,' Sadie insisted discreetly when Alejandro made no attempt to put her down. 'And I don't want to be any trouble, so if you could show me to the kitchen?' she asked the kindly-faced woman she presumed to be his housekeeper.

'Of course.'

'Maria. My housekeeper,' Alejandro gritted out, confirming Sadie's conclusion as he lowered her to the ground, having no option now but to do so, as the women made to shake hands.

'If you would like to come with me?' Maria invited, leading the way through an impressive stone archway into the house.

'My backpack—'

'Will be delivered to you in your room,' Alejandro informed her from the foot of the stairs.

As a guest she wouldn't make a fuss. As an employee, she was keen to freshen up before investigating the kitchen. She was a little bit disappointed in Alejandro's manner. Having thought him relaxed after the formality of Madrid, it seemed he could switch in an instant to being dictatorial if it suited him. It didn't suit Sadie, which was something she would have to delicately address.

His home soon distracted her. It was glorious…stunning…full of art and beautiful furniture, with a vaulted hall and marble pillars, and acres of the most exquisite stained glass. The scale was epic. And perfect for a man as complex as Alejandro, she thought.

'We'll talk again in the morning when you've had time to rest,' he informed her as he jogged past her up the stairs.

'What about your supper?' she queried.

'What about it? I eat promptly at ten. That should give you plenty of time to find your way around the kitchen and prepare something suitably delicious.' He disappeared into one of the doors leading off the hallway, shutting it firmly behind him.

With senna pods as a main ingredient, potentially, Sadie thought. Maybe she should forget Annalisa's concerns and let him starve. Alejandro might have changed from the man she'd known in Madrid, but he was still a dinosaur. If an extremely attractive relic, she concluded as he stopped on the landing and eased onto one tight hip. No one should look that good. Smouldering looks like Alejandro's belonged on the big screen, or in a fantasy where men were built like gladiators and had bodies that were invitations to sin.

Maria broke the brief awkward silence that followed Alejandro's departure with the information that she had bought cold cuts in the market, which were now in the refrigerator, and that there was also plenty of fresh fruit and vegetables in the kitchen pantry.

'This is just one of El Duque's many homes across the world,' Maria explained as they continued their tour. 'But I believe this is his favourite,' she added, 'as he always tells me how pleased he is to be back.'

It was where he felt free, Sadie thought, and who wouldn't be glad to live here? She could hardly take in each new wonder, from intricately worked rugs in a variety of jewel colours, to the art and artefacts of a type she'd only seen in museums before. It was hard to believe this was one man's home, and for only part of his time at that. 'It's absolutely beautiful,' she told Maria, 'but as I'm only here to cook, I don't think I should be staying in a guest room. I don't want to be any trouble.'

'But El Duque has insisted.' Maria said this with a shrug as if that closed the matter.

'Maybe just for tonight,' Sadie conceded, 'if that's what he wants. I won't be staying long,' she added as Alejandro's dangerously brooding expression flashed across her mind.

'We love having visitors,' Maria assured her, 'and surely you won't want to miss the party?'

'The party?' Sadie queried.

'The big, annual party.'

'I'd better be quick, and get down to the kitchen,' Sadie said, already thinking that with a party looming and the catering involved, there was no time to lose when it came to investigating what she had to work with in the kitchen.

Worryingly, Maria frowned. 'El Duque orders in. He has never hired a chef before. The kitchens here are long-neglected. He flies in caterers whenever he needs them, and they bring their own equipment on the helicopter.'

As fast as Sadie tried to absorb this, her mind filled with other questions. 'So, how does he manage to eat when he's on his own?'

'I bring food from the village and he uses an ancient microwave to heat it up.'

'A *microwave*?' Sadie's expression was one of pure shock. 'Are you sure?'

'Positive.' Maria's mouth pressed down, as if she shared Sadie's concern. 'I took delivery of the contraption myself when I first started working here. As for the rest of the equipment in the kitchen...' She frowned. 'I'm not sure if any of it works, as most of it hasn't been used for years.'

Oh, boy, thought Sadie, but Annalisa had begged her to come, and Chef Sorollo wanted those recipes, and she had no intention of letting either of them down.

'These are your rooms,' Maria explained as she turned a shining brass handle on a heavy oak door. 'I hope you'll be comfortable.'

'I'm sure I will. Thank you so much.'

'Don't thank me, thank El Duque.'

She would, but only with a good supper, Sadie thought.

Sadie, here...under his roof, just a few yards away. It seemed incredible, and was enough to throw him completely, hence his short temper. He hadn't experienced a reaction like this to a woman for as long as he could remember, maybe ever. What was it about Sadie Montgomery, when she plagued him with challenges every chance she got?

Normally so calm in the mountains, all his

gypsy passion had come to the fore, turning him into a raging bull, so impatient to introduce Sadie to this other, very different part of his life that he couldn't curb his feelings or the urge to see her again. But first, his sister had some explaining to do.

Annalisa answered his call on the first ring. 'Did she get there safely? Oh, yes…look, I got a text from Sadie saying she's there.'

'What are you playing at, Annalisa?' he demanded.

His sister hurried on, ignoring his question. 'I've been so worried. The lift I arranged for Sadie didn't materialise for some reason.'

'Well, she's here now,' he said gruffly. 'What I want to know is why.'

'Why? To redesign the kitchen, of course, and to help you with the catering for the party… It makes perfect sense.'

'Does it?' Images of Sadie swinging from a tree sprang uninvited into his mind. 'She's out of her depth here.'

'I doubt Sadie's out of her depth anywhere,' Annalisa argued.

He grunted at this. 'And when a quiet, reserved woman like Sadie Montgomery is introduced to the raw passion of flamenco, what then? Maybe I should send her home,' he added, thinking out loud.

'Because?' Annalisa queried.

'Never mind.' Because flamenco in the mountains was an untamed, visceral force that threw people together, as it had thrown his parents together. Care for the people on his land had prompted his father to visit the flamenco camp, but it was Alejandro's mother who had kept him there. There was magic in the mountains, his mother had told Alejandro when he was just a little boy. Things happened here that happened nowhere else. He'd felt that force, and he wasn't ready to have his life turned upside down by a young female chef. His duties wouldn't allow for the disturbance. Even this brief stay was an indulgence.

Annalisa was silent, which was a first for her. 'Are you all right?' he asked. The Prince, he thought, grinding his jaw.

'Butt out of my life, Alejandro,' Annalisa flashed as if reading his mind. 'Get it into your head that I'm a grown woman and quite

capable of making my own plans without sub-
mitting each of them for your approval. I love
you very much, but, honestly, sometimes you
take your responsibilities too far.'

Was that even possible? he wondered.

'Just be good to Sadie.'

He stared at the receiver in his hand as the
connection was cut. Shaking his head, he
huffed an ironic laugh at the thought that he
was besieged equally by beauty and by con-
frontation.

Is that so bad a deal?

He was about to pull away from the window
when he spotted Sadie crossing the courtyard
beneath him. She glanced up as if sensing his
interest. He held her stare and dipped his chin
briefly in acknowledgement. Was she smiling?
He couldn't tell.

CHAPTER FIVE

ON HER WAY downstairs to investigate what she had been told was the 'long-neglected' kitchen, Sadie was shocked to find 'long-neglected' an understatement. Compared to the rest of the monastery, which had been renovated to the nth degree, this was a forgotten land. The staircase leading into the bowels of the building lacked any hint of glamour. It was like going back in time, Sadie thought as she ran her hand along the cold iron bannister. Rough-hewn stone steps had remained uncarpeted, and her footsteps rattled unnervingly as she descended into the shadows.

Gothic overload, she thought as she opened a creaking door. The dank, uninviting space couldn't have differed more from the sparkling, vibrant kitchen at El Gato Feroz. Outdated was putting it mildly.

But even this unpromising start didn't daunt her. Nothing was beyond repair. Her investigations uncovered a small elevator with ropes and pulleys to transport food safely to the upper floors, and a useful, if ancient, range. She could easily make do. Everything was well cared for, thanks to Maria, and there was no better way to find out exactly what was needed during the refurbishment than to get to work on the *master's* supper right now. No senna pods in the cupboards, unfortunately, but Maria had provided an excellent selection of fresh food.

'Not up to your exacting standards, I presume?'

And breathe. Streaks of shock, excitement and wariness dashed through her in turn as she turned to face the doorway. Looking exactly like a dark angel in some Gothic story, with his thick, unruly mop of black hair catching on his 'I don't care to shave much' stubble, Alejandro, still damp and glowing from a shower or a swim, was dressed casually in jeans and a T-shirt that sculpted his incredible physique.

With his hip propped against the door, he watched her with a brooding expression on his face. 'How long have you been standing there?' she challenged as her heart beat a crazy tattoo.

'Long enough.' He straightened up, and as he prowled a little closer, he frowned. 'I believe I set a deadline.'

'You did,' she agreed. 'It might have to be something cold. I haven't tested the range yet, but I'm guessing you're hungry.'

'Always.'

Why did every word he said appear to carry multiple meanings? Was her imagination guilty of running riot, or was animal instinct to blame? Whichever it was, quivers of awareness were running up and down her spine. Acting unconcerned, she began to prepare the food. There was nothing Gothic about the cleanliness of the kitchen. Everything was spotless, and the refrigerator was full of delicious cold cuts.

'Make a list of anything you need,' Alejandro said as she foraged for ingredients. 'If you want hot food, the microwave is new, and seems to be working just fine.'

'I can't remember the last time I used a microwave.'

'This is a private home, not El Gato Feroz,' Alejandro informed her in a clipped voice. He didn't take criticism well, she thought as they exchanged determined stares.

'Am I going to eat tonight or not?' he demanded.

'Of course you are. The quality, however, will depend on how often you interfere.'

There was a tense and incredulous silence. Risking a glance, she saw that his expression had switched in an instant from impatient to hard, but there was no way of avoiding him as he made himself comfortable on a chair at the small kitchen table.

It took longer than usual to dish up an acceptable plate of food. She was still finding her way around the kitchen, while trying to avoid Alejandro! There was no answer to finding her way around his testosterone, unfortunately. He was such a potent force that his animal vitality washed over her whether she liked it or not. The kitchen was her territory, where she had always felt at home, but not this evening. She felt like a trapped animal and was bumbling around like a novice.

There was only one answer to that. Take control.

'Honey and lemon,' she said after a few minutes, pressing a steaming mug into his hand, to give those big hands something to do. 'To soothe your throat,' she explained briskly.

'My throat's healed, Doctor, but thank you very much,' he said.

She knew he was mocking her, and almost flinched when their hands brushed. So, now he knew how powerfully he affected her. The knowledge pleased him, she gathered when she saw the glint of amusement in his eyes.

'Delicious,' he murmured, holding her stare.

So, the Gypsy King was back. How quickly Alejandro could switch personas. He'd use whichever suited him in the moment, she guessed, which made him extremely dangerous, if only because she found both equally devastating. But this bad boy edged it, and they were alone.

'Now feed me,' he said, handing back the mug.

Second contact gave him another chance to see her tense and gasp as their fingers brushed.

'How do you like your eggs?' And if I don't break them over your head, I'll cook them to your liking, she thought, smiling a pleasant, professional smile.

'Cooked in the open air,' he said with a shrug.

'Don't joke. It might come to that,' she said with a glance around the dilapidated kitchen.

'I'm not joking. Have you written that list yet?'

'I've been busy preparing your meal.' Lifting the plate, she practically shoved it in his chest. How she didn't upend it over his gloriously handsome head remained a mystery. His brow quirked. His hard mouth almost smiled. Good. Maybe he'd got the message that she was a professional woman, not a doormat.

Having cleaned his plate, he pushed it away and looked up. 'Be ready to leave for the flamenco camp in the morning. Not what you expected?' he asked when she remained silent.

'Actually, no. I expected you to say thank you.'

Fire flashed in his eyes. 'We leave at dawn,' he rapped, standing.

'And my list?'

'I'll read it when I get a chance. But you have to write it first,' he pointed out.

'I have it logged in my head.'

'And what will this new equipment cost me?'

'Far less than eating out.'

'You have an answer for everything, *señorita.*'

'In my job I need to,' she said.

As she leaned over to take his plate, they almost collided. It was like a game of cat and mouse, and she had no doubt as to the role she was playing. She gasped out loud when Alejandro caught hold of her arms. 'You seem determined to tease me, *señorita.*'

'I can assure you, it's entirely unintentional.' Staring down at his hand on her arm, she waited until he released her.

He did so, but then he drew her back again

with a grip that was both gentle and compelling. 'Put the plate down,' he said.

Neatly sidestepping, she put it in the sink. Turning, she found him behind her. She was sure he was going to kiss her. And he did. Politely, on both cheeks.

'Thank you, *señorita*, for a delicious snack.'

She could have kicked herself for being so naive. What an idiot to think he'd make a move. Alejandro was so much older and more experienced, he was just laughing at her. He knew what she was thinking and what she'd expected, and to think her feelings were an open book was almost more concerning than the prospect of a trip to a remote encampment in the mountains.

'Be ready at dawn,' he reminded her as he turned and walked away.

Back in his suite of rooms, Alejandro lifted his crystal brandy glass in a toast to a most satisfactory skirmish. Sadie's disappointment when he'd kissed her on the cheek told him everything, but she was gutsy and defiant, and he liked that. He liked Sadie more and more.

Guessing she'd still be in the kitchen compiling her list, he lifted the house phone. It took her a while to answer. He guessed she was probably exploring long-forgotten cupboards.

'Hello?'

She sounded surprised to hear from him. 'Maybe I was a bit short,' he conceded on the basis that a strong woman would fight him every inch of the way, and that it would be more pleasurable to extend that fight until it landed them in bed. 'I just wanted to confirm that you have carte blanche to improve the kitchen—whatever you need will be helicoptered in.'

'Thank you.' There was a pause, and then she said, 'You'll have my list in the morning. I hope you've got a big helicopter, by the way.'

'Enormous,' he confirmed, deadpan.

There was an electric silence, and then she asked, 'Are you mocking me?'

'Would I?'

'Oh, yes, I think so. Is that all? Only I have work to do.'

She was dismissing him? With a silent laugh, he bid her goodnight. Some might think him changeable depending on the circumstance, but Sadie's unique blend of professional confidence and personal insecurity continued to intrigue him. The hunger to know more about her was growing by the hour. Once she was away from her duties in the very different setting of the flamenco camp, it would be interesting to see if she changed too.

Sadie had never seen a live flamenco show, let alone visited an encampment in the mountains devoted to the art. She didn't know what to expect and was excited. Alejandro had explained as they set out on horseback that professional artistes came from all over the world to study at the camp so they could hone their craft and pass on the artistry.

The steep mountain track finally opened onto a wider trail that led, in turn, to a surprising plateau that housed what she could only describe as a hidden city in the mountains, where gaily painted caravans had replaced the more traditional snow-white houses in the village. Deep caves were carved into a menacing rock face at one side of this heavily populated carpet of green, while craggy, snow-capped peaks clawed at the sky above them, but what surprised Sadie most of all was how warm it was.

'The flamenco camp enjoys a microclimate,' Alejandro explained when she asked the question, 'which was why it was set up here.'

The hidden city was a bustling place, and their arrival caused a great deal of excitement. The Gypsy King had returned from his travels, Sadie concluded as crowds began to mass along the way. She could see now where Alejandro got his good looks. The dark flashing eyes and glossy black hair of his people were unmistakable. He was one of them, imperious and proud with incredible bone structure. He had the same hawkish stare, chiselled features and stern, authoritative air. A group of men came forward to lead his horse into camp, and they talked in a language she didn't recognise. Alejandro slipped easily into this new, exotic tongue. A Spanish duke, who was equally at home in the mountains as in the salons of Madrid, with a gypsy princess mother and an aristocratic father. How could his history be any more fascinating? She almost preferred this rougher, far more dangerous-looking man than the polished Don, who all but ruled in Madrid. The downside was that she felt like a mouse in her jeans and nondescript top. If she'd known there would be such a welcome—she'd still be wearing jeans and a nondescript top. This welcome was for Alejandro, a man who made her senses riot.

Tensing, she held her breath as Alejandro insisted on lifting her down from the horse. In those few seconds, she was aware of everything about him: his heat, his potency, his outrageous good looks and the warm, clean man smell he exuded.

'Would you like to dance?' he asked, noticing her staring at the stage.

'Like this?' She grimaced as she stared down at her workmanlike clothes.

'Why not?' He flashed a look that seared her from the inside out.

'Better not. I'll only tread on your toes.'

'What I meant,' he explained, 'was, would you like to take a flamenco class?'

He really was the expert in making her

cheeks blaze red. 'I have two left feet and no sense of rhythm,' she said, recovering fast.

'Have you ever put that to the test?'

The expression in Alejandro's eyes made his simple enquiry sound like the most dangerous suggestion. Her imagination working over-time again, Sadie conceded. 'Okay,' she said in the spirit of keeping things cool between them. 'I'll have a go.'

'Would you like some help?' Alejandro asked with the faintest of smiles.

'I'm guessing I'm going to need some help,' she said as her body begged her to let him try.

Yet again, he had wrong-footed her. Calling to one of the attractive sloe-eyed beauties, he asked the woman to help Sadie learn the steps.

The young woman introduced herself. 'My name is Marissa, Sadie. Please come with me. I think you need an outfit first to put you in the mood.'

It would take more than a dress and a pair of castanets to help her out, Sadie thought, but the excitement of being invited into one of the beautifully decorated caravans really helped her to forget her embarrassment at misunderstanding Alejandro's suggestion.

Marissa was so easy to get along with that they were soon chatting easily. It turned out they had a lot in common. They were both ambitious, and both equally wary of men—Sadie because her childhood had been so unhappy, forced to watch her father beating her mother when he was drunk, and Marissa because, she explained to Sadie, she was so unlucky in love.

The compact space was packed with clothes in every colour of the rainbow, hanging on rails and spilling out of wooden trunks. 'Sit down,' Marissa invited, 'while I find you something to wear. Who needs men when we have music and dance, lots of clothes and good food? Let them ride their horses, and fight and swear. We know what matters, don't we?'

Love, Sadie thought as she sat down on the small sofa while Marissa rifled through the various options on the rail. Love mattered, though friendship mattered hugely too, and for some reason she felt confident she and Marissa would become firm friends. There was something about the other woman that seemed familiar. She was certainly warm and couldn't have been more welcoming.

'I'm glad Alejandro brought you to us,' she said, turning to smile at Sadie. 'He is regarded as our King, but I'm lucky enough to call him brother.'

'Your brother,' Sadie exclaimed, realising now why Marissa seemed vaguely familiar.

'We had different fathers, but the same mother,' Marissa explained. 'My parents were childhood sweethearts. I was born when my mother was barely eighteen. My parents broke up when she met Alejandro's father. The price she had to pay was leaving me with my father's family in the mountains. No one could have predicted that Alejandro would grow up to be a man who loved me as his sister from the start. I couldn't have a better brother if I searched the entire world.'

Time passed swiftly as they chatted on, until Sadie realised they'd been talking for over an hour. Alejandro was with his friends and wouldn't miss her, and just being with Marissa had made her feel confident in this

new and very different environment, so it was
time well spent.

'For me?' she exclaimed with pleasure when
Marissa decided Sadie should wear a fabulous
turquoise skirt. Heavily decorated with gold
embroidery, it looked amazing with the fine
white lace blouse she chose to go with it.

'This will suit your colouring,' Marissa
promised as she held it up.

It would certainly showcase her assets, Sadie
thought with amusement. The fabric was so
fine it was completely see-through, and the
flimsy garment tied in a bow at the neck, leaving very little to the imagination.

'You wear it like this,' Marissa said, dem-
onstrating how the neckline should sit off the
shoulders. 'Provocative, huh?' She laughed.
'I used to work in an office in Madrid, so I
know how it is there, but when you're here...'
Marissa grinned. 'Anything goes.'

'Isn't there anything more discreet?' Sadie
asked, losing courage briefly when she viewed
her profile in the mirror.

'Are you kidding?' Marissa exclaimed. 'Why
aim for discreet when you can achieve fabu-

lous? Or are you afraid of causing *too* much interest?'

'I'm not afraid.' Sadie laughed. 'But I do work for Alejandro, and I don't want him to get the wrong idea.'

'Are you sure?' Marissa's eyes twinkled. 'I've seen the way he looks at you. I can't believe you're not lovers yet.'

'Whoa!' Sadie exclaimed. 'Not lovers ever,' she assured her new friend.

With a shrug, Marissa smiled. 'If you say so.'

'I most certainly do say so,' Sadie insisted, but then they both broke into laughter, and the moment was forgotten in the excitement of wearing such colourful and glamorous clothes.

'And wear your hair loose,' Marissa advised as she cast a critical eye over her protégée's appearance. 'For me, it is different,' she added, as she smoothed her neatly pinned hair. 'I'm taking lessons, while you're—'

'Not taking lessons,' Sadie confirmed dryly. 'I'm here to learn about recipes.'

'Of course you are,' Marissa agreed, straight-faced.

'No, really, I am—' She gasped as Marissa plucked out the pins from Sadie's hair and ran her fingers through the gleaming red-gold locks.

'That should generate some interest,' Marissa commented as she stood back to admire her handiwork. 'Alejandro will certainly notice you now.'

'That is not what I want,' Sadie said firmly, wondering whom she was trying to convince.

'Then, it should be,' Marissa insisted with a mischievous grin. 'My brother is the most eligible bachelor in Spain. Take a look at yourself in the mirror. You should never tie your hair back. He's going to go mad when he sees you.'

Sadie couldn't believe the transformation and wasn't sure she had the confidence to pull it off.

'You look great,' Marissa insisted, seeing her uncertainty. 'Come on—we've wasted enough time in here already.'

So, she'd try out the new look on Alejandro, and let him try and mock her if he dared.

CHAPTER SIX

HE RODE BACK into camp just as Sadie stepped out of one of the oldest and most beautifully renovated caravans, where his sister Marissa kept her prized wardrobe collection. His reaction was sheer incredulity, mixed with a very primal urge to stake his claim on a woman who couldn't have looked more incredible if she'd tried. Ditching jeans for a traditional flamenco outfit had brought about the most unbelievable transformation, turning Sadie from hot into stunning.

He took his horse to rub it down. It had been a short but vigorous ride with his friends, and the animals were steaming. The men gave no quarter, and he'd found the fast pace invigorating. His hackles rose when he realised his companions had also noticed Sadie. How could they not when her figure was shown to best advantage in the clothes she was wearing, with her unusual hair glittering in the sun as it cascaded to her waist in a thick fall of shimmering, fiery waves? Who wouldn't want to tangle their hands through that? A group of admiring youths were starting to show her attention, he noticed, and some things were too special to lose. Having settled his horse, he bid goodbye to his friends.

Sadie had joined the team carrying platters and bowls for that evening's feast to rough-hewn tables erected in front of the stage. She could feel Alejandro watching her as intently as she had watched him ride into camp. He looked every bit the Gypsy King, with his thick black hair barely tamed beneath a black bandana. The heat of his stare shot fire through every fibre of her being. She'd had enough! Turning suddenly, she levelled a stare at his arrogant face, only to have her heart go crazy when he acknowledged the challenge with an amused dip of his head.

His bronzed and muscular arms remained folded across the impressive width of his chest as he continued to stare at her, while low-slung jeans, secured by a heavy-duty belt, drew her gaze where it absolutely shouldn't wander.

'Are you okay?' Marissa asked, snapping Sadie out of the trance. 'Do you need some help with those dishes?'

Sadie had stalled on the path with her arms laden with platters of food, she realised now.

'Oh, I get it,' Marissa added in a voice ringing with humour. 'My brother's distracting you!'

'Don't be silly.' Even to Sadie's ears her laugh sounded unconvincing. 'I'm here to collect recipes and organise your brother's kitchen…and absolutely nothing else. What?' she queried, when Marissa cocked her chin to give Sadie a disbelieving look.

'I've never heard lust described as organising a man's kitchen before,' Marissa admitted. 'I hope you get his pots and pans in order soon.'

It was good to see the two women laughing together. Sadie had fitted into camp life well. Heat surged between them as he stared at her and she stared back. *She wanted him.* Animal instinct, always a close ally, told him that. But delay was good, though it could turn into the very real physical pain he was suffering now. Even so, he wouldn't rush her. Sadie would come to him in her own time, and he was tired of easy conquests. She was unique in that she was both refreshing and a challenge, and she couldn't care less if he was a duke, a billionaire or a stevedore from the docks. Added to which, for the first time in his life, the outcome of any approach he made was uncertain—which only made the challenge of Sadie Montgomery all the more appealing.

He strolled across the camp to join the two women, and was only halfway to his goal when Marissa, seeing what he was about to do, slipped away, leaving him and Sadie alone. Straightening up, she lifted her chin to stare him in the eyes, as if demanding *he* explain himself. What was the situation? Sadie's straightforward expression seemed to ask. Were they a duke and a professional chef, or simply a man and a woman? He knew which he preferred.

'Join me at my table,' he said as he halted in front of her.

'I'm going to dance with Marissa first,' she told him, 'and then I can only sit down when everyone else has eaten.'

'Can't you forget your duties for once?'

'Do you forget yours?'

'Never,' he confirmed, thinking her the most infuriating woman he'd ever met, as well as the most appealing. 'When you're ready, come and sit with me,' he tempered, feeling confident that she would.

'If there's space at your table, I will,' she said.

'There will be space,' he assured her. This was torture. From a distance the traditional clothes had made Sadie appear alluring, but this close up they made her irresistible. 'Our flamenco clothes suit you.'

'Thank you,' she said, and without further ado she left him to continue serving the food.

'Annoying woman,' he breathed as she walked away. The urge to know Sadie more intimately was eating him alive. Adaptable and capable, she appealed in every way. Her self-control was admirable, which led to the next question: would self-control desert her when his hands touched her naked body?

He could think of nothing else throughout the meal. No woman had ever preoccupied his thoughts as she did. When his sister and Sadie left the table arm in arm, he felt pushed out. But not for long. Fingers snapped and feet were already stamping out a rhythm as old as time as the musicians began to tune up. Rising from his seat, he strode up to Sadie. 'Dance with me.' His tone was abrupt, and his expression must have been a thundercloud at the thought that she might say no.

'Why not?' she said.

Her cheeks were flushed from all the rushing about, and her lips were full and moist from the juice she'd been drinking. She walked towards him with all the dignity of a gypsy queen and moved into his arms as if she belonged there. But then she tensed.

Why must the past intrude now? Sadie wondered tensely as she stiffened in Alejandro's arms. Because the past could not be so easily dismissed, she concluded as an icy shiver gripped her. Just because she was in a different place with different people, didn't mean that childhood memories would simply float away. She had to fight them, she determined, or be crushed.

'I'm…just worried about treading on your toes,' she lied when Alejandro, sensing the change in her, asked if she was okay.

'Let me worry about that,' he said, drawing her closer still.

Gradually and incredibly, she began to relax. The magic of the music, she supposed. Now she could appreciate every contour of his body…and what a body.

'Stop worrying about the steps,' he advised in a husky whisper that tickled her ear. 'Just let the music take you where you need to be.'

That could be dangerous, Sadie thought as a quiver of arousal snatched the breath from her lungs, but somehow Alejandro made her forget the danger of being in his arms and concentrate on steps that had looked so intricate but, with him guiding her, suddenly became possible. The deeper she delved into the intoxicating culture of his people, the further her neatly ordered life in Madrid slipped away.

'And now you dance for me,' he said as the musicians began to play a wild tarantella and everyone whooped.

'When you cook for me, I'll dance for you,' she fired back.

He laughed. 'Touché. We'll dance together.'

Everyone was watching them, Sadie realised. They had been on the dance floor quite some time, and it was bound to cause interest when the Gypsy King danced with his young female chef. Feeling suddenly exposed and on show, she pulled away, only to have Alejandro bring her back. It was all too easy to fall under his spell as she stared into his eyes. She was soft and he was hard. They were complete opposites but, like two sides of the same coin, it felt as if they were meant to be together.

The next melody wound its way around her heart. It was a slow, plangent tune that made her yearn to belong somewhere, and to someone. Alejandro's brazenly sexual body pressed against hers only added to the ache inside her heart. The musky scent of horse and leather and warm, clean man clung to him, driving her senses wild. She had never imagined feeling this sense of belonging in any man's arms, but even that was dangerous. She had always avoided rejection by never getting too close to anything or anyone. The one exception to that rule, until just a short time ago, was Chef Sorollo, and yet now she was in danger of falling in love with Alejandro and his people.

Face facts. You don't belong here and never will.

Breaking free, she threaded her way through the dancing couples without looking back, only knowing that she needed space from a man who possessed the power to lay her emotions bare.

The sounds of celebration were soon left behind, and Sadie found herself clambering over rocks, not really knowing where she was heading. Hitting a patch of shale, she slid out of control for several moments, and was badly shaken up by the time she finally managed to dig her heels in and slide to a sitting halt. Only then did she see the lights of the village twinkling far below her, and a looming precipice just feet away. The drop must have been a thousand feet or more. Whimpering with shock, she planted her hands behind her to act as an anchor, and, inch by torturous inch, she slowly dragged herself back up the treacherous slope.

'You little fool!'

Strong arms yanked her to her feet. Senses heightened in that instant, and she noticed everything, from the wind in her face, to the scent of the moss beneath her feet and the rustle of the leaves in the sparsely furnished trees above her. And above all, the fury of the man in whose arms she was being held securely.

'If I hadn't followed you—'

Clearly fighting an inner battle between rage and relief, Alejandro swung her off the ground. He was furious, while she was shivering uncontrollably at the thought of what might have happened if he hadn't come along.

'What made you think it was safe to go exploring in the dark on mountains you're unfamiliar with? Must I put you on a lead rein?' he demanded.

Knowing she'd made a fool of herself, she said nothing.

'Can you walk back to camp, or must I carry you?'

'I can walk.' She might have lost her sense of direction, but she had lost none of her determination to stand on her own.

'Are you sure?' he asked in a gentler tone that made her hesitate.

'Certain,' she bit out, fighting back the alluring thought of having someone to rely on, someone to trust completely, a homeport where she would always feel safe. If she allowed Alejandro to coddle her, she might start to believe all sorts of things, and that could only make her weak.

'I'll show you around in daylight,' he promised grimly. 'Until then, you stay in camp.'

'I've kept you away from your friends long enough.' She longed to escape the piercing stare that seemed to see right into her soul, which was brimful with insecurities already, before she had just added to them with more.

'They can live without me. I'd rather make sure you're okay. You're still shaking.'

'I'll be better on my own,' she insisted on a tight throat.

'You don't know that, and I'm not going to give you chance to find out. This will be your last adventure for tonight.'

She felt like a child being scolded, but she was in the wrong, and had no clue about a safe route back. 'Just show me the way and I'll follow you.'

Alejandro started off, but the fall had taken more out of her than she expected.

It was lucky his reflexes were whip-fast, allowing him to catch her before she hit the ground. 'I'm not waiting for you to decide how you'll get back to camp,' he assured her, and with that he swung her into his arms.

How had an evening that started so well ended like this? Sadie wondered. She'd never been so confident away from her beloved kitchen, or so happy, and now she just felt like a chump. She was also extremely aware of Alejandro's powerful body as he carried her along as if she weighed nothing in a grip that was both secure and unthreatening. In spite of all her hang-ups, she wanted to know him better. Was that wrong? Was that dangerous? And had she blown any chance of that happening now? Would the fact that they were, quite literally, worlds apart remain an impenetrable barrier?

'Could you let me down?' she asked when they arrived back in camp.

'No. I'm taking you to Marissa's caravan, and making sure you go inside.'

So much for romance, Sadie thought dryly, but why would he want to be with such a numbskull, when Alejandro could have any woman he wanted? Spain's most eligible bachelor, Marissa had called him. 'I'd like to go back to the party, if only to prove I can get through the rest of the evening without a hitch.'

Thumbing his sharp black stubble as he regarded her through narrowed eyes, Alejandro observed, 'You were staggering with shock only minutes ago, so go to bed and give yourself chance to recover.'

Her fantasies about the Gypsy King and the innocent chef were truly misguided, Sadie reasoned as Alejandro took her by the arm to steer her towards Marissa's caravan. He had zero tolerance, and while she found his decisive nature attractive, it put him firmly in the 'Don't go there' category. She couldn't guarantee that she wouldn't make a few more blunders before her work was finished in the mountains, and she could only prove a disappointment to such a connoisseur of women.

And she had more sense, Sadie reassured herself as Alejandro, having handed her over to Marissa, returned to his group of friends and slipped easily into conversation, as if nothing unusual had occurred on the tranquil, starry night.

CHAPTER SEVEN

MARISSA WAS MORE than happy for Sadie to spend the night in her caravan and was careful not to ask questions unless Sadie offered the information…such as why she had disappeared in the middle of the party.

'I went exploring and got myself into a spot of bother. Luckily, your brother found me before I took the shortcut to the village.'

'Over the cliff?' Marissa's hand shot to her mouth. 'Never wander around here in the dark. I know it all looks so homey and safe, but that's only because the camp is located on a plateau. There are dangers all around. If you stray far, any one of us could get into trouble.'

'Don't I know it,' Sadie agreed as she sipped her late-night drink of hot milk, which Marissa had insisted would help her to sleep.

'Did my brother upset you?' Marissa asked

as she plonked herself down on the narrow twin bed next to Sadie's. 'Is that why you left?'

'No. I managed this all by myself,' Sadie admitted, pulling a face. 'I was just lucky that Alejandro realised I was heading into trouble, and decided to follow me—'

'Wait a minute…didn't my brother find you on the trail the first time around? Weren't you hooked onto a tree? This is becoming a dangerous habit, and one you must break. He might not always be around to save you.'

'I don't expect him to be around. I should think he's had enough of me by now.'

Marissa laughed. 'I've known Alejandro all his life, and if he spends any time with you at all, he's interested.'

'I think he tolerates me, and then only barely,' Sadie admitted.

'Well, next time, let me show you around. I would have liked to join you.'

'In jumping over a cliff?' Sadie suggested wryly. They both laughed, and then she added, 'And as for your brother? He's a lot more than I could handle.'

'Would you like to? Handle him, I mean,' Marissa teased.

When they had finished laughing, Marissa gutsily, and Sadie pretending she was taking all this in her stride, Marissa insisted, 'You do like him. You're just not ready to admit it yet...maybe not even to yourself.'

'Are you trying to set me up with him?'

'Me?' Marissa widened her eyes. 'Whatever makes you think that?'

'The circumstantial evidence is overwhelming?' Sadie suggested with a grin.

'So, I like you,' Marissa admitted with a smile and a shrug. 'What are you going to do about it?'

'You *like* me, and your way of showing this is to throw me in your brother's path?'

'He's not so bad. Don't believe everything you hear about him. And from what you say, you threw yourself in his path. As for my feelings on the subject?' Marissa pulled a comic face. 'Alejandro needs bringing into line, and you're the best hope I've got.'

Sadie couldn't pretend she wasn't thrilled to have Marissa's approval, but she had to tell her the truth. 'I'm not sure I'm qualified. My experience of men is practically nil.'

'Yes, you are,' Marissa insisted with more force than Sadie expected. 'You're a gutsy woman who knows exactly what's going on.'

'I wish—'

'Don't tell me you can't see what's happening between you and Alejandro,' Marissa insisted. 'If you walk away from him now, you might regret it for the rest of your life.'

Sadie sighed and shook her head. 'How can you know that?'

Flicking her hair back, Marissa fixed an intent stare on Sadie's face. 'Forget what you think you know about our people reading tarot cards, tea leaves and crystal balls, because nothing on this earth can ever come close to a woman's intuition.'

The night after rescuing Sadie felt like the longest night of his life. He was up at dawn to go riding, and when he cantered back into camp and saw Sadie with some of the older members of the community gathered around her, he reined in, transfixed. She looked so fresh and natural, friendly and warm, as if nothing untoward had happened last night to rattle her professional persona. She was as adept at switching between professional and personal as he was.

Having watched for a while, he sprang down from the saddle. Not once had she glanced across, and a very primal part of him wanted her as acutely conscious of him as he was of her. He led his horse over to the group, where he discovered they were sharing family recipes. How long would that take? After a restless night, staring out of his caravan window at stars that seemed close enough to grab hold of, he was impatient to be alone with Sadie.

'Good morning,' Sadie said politely, glancing up at last.

A happy chorus of '*Buenos días*, Don Alegon,' chimed out from people he loved, all of whom he acknowledged warmly, while wanting Sadie to stop what she was doing and pay attention to him. But that would not be Sadie, and he admired her dedication even when it led to delay. Just as she had in the kitchen of El Gato Feroz, she was concentrating on the current situation, which, in this case, included the people around her. If she included him in the discussion, it was in the same interested and informative manner that she spoke to everyone else. He couldn't help but smile inwardly as he watched and waited. What he had really wanted when he arrived back from his ride, he conceded, was for Sadie to rush over and throw her arms around him. What she did was pass around a tray of freshly baked lemon cakes for everyone to try.

'These *magdalenas* are good,' he commented.

'Top-quality ingredients and careful preparation,' Sadie informed him in her no-nonsense cook's voice.

'Preparation is vital to any task,' he replied straight-faced.

He saw by a flicker in her eyes that she knew exactly what he was talking about, but she continued on with her class unfazed.

'Each and every dish deserves to be developed to its full potential,' she told the group surrounding her, but her gaze lingered on him. 'Don't you agree, Don Alegon?'

'Absolutely,' he said.

The staring standoff lasted a few moments more, and then she carried on, until eventually the class ended and her students drifted away.

'You seem to have made yourself at home here,' he remarked.

'I can't help myself. I love it here. Apart from El Gato Feroz, I've never truly felt that I belonged.'

'And before that?'

'Before that, I was like tumbleweed, going wherever life took me. A fairly restricted life as a child should have warned me that life on a super-yacht wasn't for me, but I tried it, and it was there that I did my first professional cooking, so no experience is ever truly wasted. I love the freedom here, and I love the open-mindedness of the people.' Her shoulders lifted and fell as she admitted, 'I'm happy.'

'And you seem to have made quite an impression,' he observed, seeing the knots of people chatting together and shooting admiring glances at Sadie.

'I just love to share,' she said, 'and so do

your people. I really enjoy my work, and I enjoy learning from them.'

He couldn't imagine Sadie ever being selfish with her knowledge. Her natural warmth wouldn't allow it.

'Sadie?' he prompted when she felt silent.

'I haven't always been able to share,' she admitted. 'When I lived at home my opinions were considered worthless.'

'So you kept it all in, and saved it for us,' he said gently. He could see from her face this was going too fast, and that she hadn't meant to mention her childhood, so he backed off. 'Have you eaten anything yet?'

'No,' she admitted. 'Have you?'

'I'm about to... I hope,' he prompted.

'Ah,' she said, smiling, 'that was a hint. I'll feed you,' she offered, with a wide-eyed innocent assurance that made his groin tighten to the point of pain. He, to his ultimate discredit, could think of nothing but Sadie, stripped of her chef's jacket and jeans, under him.

She got busy and had soon prepared two delicious plates of food. This was a very different woman from the woman he'd danced with last night. There was no shining hair flying free, or alluring clothes to tease his senses. Right now, Sadie Montgomery was the consummate professional, with severely scraped-back hair and a jacket so stiff it could stand on its own. He admired her for her dedication, and the sheer hard work it had taken to reach such a high standard in her chosen profession, but he missed wild Sadie more.

'You know what they say about all work and no play,' he commented when he'd finished every scrap on his plate.

She stared at him levelly as she collected up his plate with hers. 'Success?'

Huffing a laugh, he conceded the point with a nod.

'What are you suggesting?' she asked as he helped her clear up.

'That I introduce you to this area properly, so there are no more exciting incidents in the middle of the night.'

'There won't be another,' she assured him, holding his stare. Then suddenly, and apparently for no reason he could fathom, she relented. 'D'you know? I'd like that. Thank you.

Give me ten minutes to change out of these clothes.'

'Five,' he countered.

It amused him to see her eyes flash a warning, as if to say, Don't push your luck, mister. But her inner feelings gave her away and her cheeks flushed red, as if spending time with him wasn't entirely unappealing. Let your hair down, Sadie, he thought as she hurried away.

She joined Alejandro at the pony lines where he was busy saddling up two horses for them to ride out on. 'Thank you for offering to show me around,' she said, her tone formal to counter the fact that her entire being was reacting wildly to the sight of Alejandro with muscles flexing in his powerful forearms as he checked the girth on her horse.

'You're not my employee now,' he said, straightening up, 'so no need to thank me. This is your free time, and you can do as you like. I know you're interested in this very different way of life. It was the same for my father, so that's something I'm sensitive to, and can help you with.'

Alejandro's brooding expression made Sadie's heart beat even faster. She tried to concentrate on the actual, like the fact that his concern for her had drawn parallel lines above his strong nose on his ridiculously handsome face, but that only made her want him more. Then her gaze wandered to his eyes, only to find him watching her intently. To distract herself she made a fuss of the nearest horse.

'My father loved the mountains,' he went on, as he lowered her stirrups and indicated it was time to mount up. 'From his first day at the flamenco camp he was in love with everything here. It was so different from Madrid, he told me years later.'

'I know what he means, and you do too.'

'And I know that you love horses,' Alejandro commented as she scratched beneath the chin of her friendly bay gelding in a quick getting-to-know-you session before she mounted up.

'Riding was always my passion,' she admitted, 'though I don't get much chance now.' One of the few things Sadie remembered with pleasure about her childhood was her trips to the riding stables, where the horses showed more interest in her than her parents ever had.

'Will we be going anywhere where I can collect some more recipes?' she asked, conscious
of Alejandro's stare hot on her face.

'No,' he said bluntly. 'This is time off for
you. What there will be is a chance for you to
pull away from work.'

'Will you do the same?' she countered.

He paused a long moment and then said,
'Yes.'

'Then, I will too,' she agreed.

The look they shared trickled through her
senses like warm honey on a crumpet sweet-
ening everything it touched. 'I only hope I can
keep up with you,' she said, taking a look at
the black stallion Alejandro was tacking up.

'Going on past experience, I've no doubt you
will,' he told her dryly with a quick glance her
way. Springing lightly into the saddle, he led
the way.

Quite a few people waved them off as they
left the camp. There would be comment but
no unkind gossip, Sadie suspected. Everyone
was too warm for that. And, nothing ventured,
nothing gained, she decided, so whatever Alejandro's motive in asking her to join him on

the ride, she was up for it, and keen to see more of the magnificent mountains he called home.

'You're a really good rider,' he said, having tested her at a slow pace, and then speeding up to a safe, collected canter.

'This is fabulous,' Sadie called out as she urged her horse on. 'I never thought I'd get this chance, and I'm loving every minute of it.'

The scenery was stunning, and they had progressed to a gallop across the flat carpet of green, surrounded by mountains with previously hidden lakes revealing themselves in all their glittering splendour. The air was clean and sharp with the tang of ice and history, and the temperature was mild and comfortable for riding. Keeping a safe seat on a horse had all come back to her, and the bay gelding Alejandro had chosen for her to ride was kind and responsive to Sadie's smallest command.

And Alejandro?

He looked amazing. He was so easy in the saddle and rode as if he were sitting in an armchair. Totally stunning in just a casual shirt with the sleeves rolled back, and another pair of old jeans that had definitely seen better days, he could seriously derail a woman's life. If she allowed him to, Sadie reasoned. So, relax. It wasn't going to happen. She had a career she loved, and a life in Madrid.

'Still okay?' he asked, turning to stare at her as he slowed the pace.

'Loving it,' she confirmed with a smile. There was a companionship in riding together that couldn't be explained. It was something about the union between animal and human that healed the soul, she decided.

Eventually, he reined in a few yards in front of a rocky trail. 'I want to make sure you feel confident before we tackle the more testing part of this ride.'

Alejandro was the only testing part of this ride, she thought. 'I'm sure I'll be fine if we take it slowly.'

They stared at each other briefly. 'Take it at your own pace,' he said. 'If you're not happy, I'll stop. I'll ride ahead and you follow me.'

'Okay, on this one occasion,' she teased.

Turning, Alejandro flashed a smile that warmed her through, and then they were climbing steadily up the mountain, which gave her chance to appreciate a rear view that was as good as his front. He looked far more like a swarthy brigand, seated astride his snorting stallion, than a Spanish grandee on a well-schooled Arabian steed.

There was plenty more to distract her as their horses picked a cautious route up the trail. Dragging greedily on the crisp mountain air, she soaked in the incredible view around her, and in front of her, where the man with the powerful back, and shoulders wide enough to hoist an ox, was controlling his wilful stallion with the lightest touch of his long, lean legs. El Duque had never looked more satanically lustworthy than he did in the saddle, surrounded by the mountains he loved. Wherever this trail led, she would embrace each new experience with the same enthusiasm she felt for everything else.

CHAPTER EIGHT

THEY VISITED SEVERAL outlying villages, where he introduced Sadie around but avoided mentioning where she worked, or the food for which she was famous. He was serious about keeping her mind off her work. In the last place they stopped, two elderly ladies insisted on preparing a picnic for them, as if they were lovers on a day out rather than virtual strangers who would like to know each other better, and who lost no opportunity to engage in banter and challenge.

The ground was flat around the village, and he set a brisk pace when they left. 'Keep up,' he called over his shoulder.

'Or else?' Sadie countered with a laugh that was swept away by the wind.

'You'll be left behind,' he warned, though he doubted Sadie's competitive spirit would allow that to happen.

'So there you are,' he yelled as she rode alongside. 'Not bad.'

'Praise coming from you?' she yelled back.

'I must be getting careless,' he confessed with a laugh.

Her enjoyment of riding was obvious. He could tell she felt free, and, like him, Sadie's concerns faded in the mountains. Those concerns would have to be dealt with eventually, but for now, with their horses straining every muscle to gallop flat out, they were on fire with the thrill of the race, and all other considerations would have to wait.

Eventually, he stopped on the banks of a fast-moving river. 'You kept up,' he commented dryly as she dismounted.

'And you didn't fall off,' she countered with a cheeky smile. 'What if I'd fallen off? Would you have noticed?'

'Apart from the earth tremors?' he queried.

'Your gallantry does you credit,' she shot back as she ran up the stirrups.

'Do you need wrapping in cotton wool? You never gave me that impression.'

'I can hold my own,' she assured him. 'You

gave me a good horse to ride. All I had to do was give him his head and stay on. He did the rest.'

'I'm glad you approve.'

'Oh, I do,' she said. 'Picnic?' she reminded him as she unfastened the straps on the pannier holding the feast the elderly ladies had prepared for them. 'You must be hungry—I know I am.'

'Starving,' he confirmed. 'Towels,' he added, tossing a big blue one to Sadie as he produced a couple from his saddlebags. 'I used to swim here as a boy.'

'We're going to swim?' she asked, staring at the fast-moving water in alarm. 'Isn't that glacier melt?'

'Are you chicken?'

'Are you?'

'Let's cool down, then,' he proposed.

'Soon. Let's eat first.' Removing her horse's saddle, she gave him a look. 'Your childhood must have been idyllic,' she said as he helped her to set out the picnic.

'I was certainly a challenge for my parents,' he admitted.

'I can imagine,' she said.

'Stick the wine between those rocks to chill it,' he told her, handing the bottle over.

'You think of everything,' she commented with a grin.

Believe it, he thought.

They ate sparingly, and, with a swim ahead of them, barely touched the wine, and then it was a case of waiting for a while after eating, to make sure neither of them got a cramp in the icy water. Sadie hunkered down on the grass, while he lay back alongside her, resting on his elbows. She seemed reluctant to talk, so he started the conversation. 'My parents were madly in love…'

'And what a setting for it,' she commented as she looked around.

'I was lucky. They gave me the best of examples for what constitutes a happy family life.'

'So, why have you never married?'

He stared at her with amusement. 'Why are you interested?'

'I'm not,' she assured him just a little too hotly.

'It must have been a hideous loss when they were killed,' she said, changing the subject fast.

He didn't want to talk about it, but this was typical of Sadie. Where angels feared to tread she walked straight in. And only out of kindness, he reminded himself as he relaxed. It was a long time, if ever, that anyone had dared to mention the loss of his parents to him, or to Annalisa. After all these years, the wound was still red raw. Perhaps it always would be. It had certainly affected his approach to life, and especially to any potential relationship. He was wary of commitment, wary of love, because it was too much to lose. Adoring his parents as he had had made the pain of their loss almost unmanageable. Only caring for Annalisa, and building the business so many depended on, had helped him to carry on.

'You don't know what you've got until it's gone,' he murmured pensively.

It was a relief to discover that Sadie knew when to let the silence hang.

Sadie hadn't expected Alejandro to open up as he had, and this softer side of him touched her deeply. It was the first time he'd mentioned feelings, let alone allowed his mask to slip. Pain was etched on a face that usually held nothing but confidence and command. He must have bottled up everything for years, she realised, as she had.

'Annalisa's lucky to have such a wonderful brother,' she said gently.

Lifting his head, Alejandro stared her steadily in the eyes. 'I love my sister, and I'll always try to help her out, though my help isn't always wanted,' he admitted with an amused smile. 'I just hope she finds someone to care for her as I do, one day.'

'What about the Prince?'

'That milksop?' Alejandro's expression hardened. 'I'll be interested to see how long he lasts. I just hope he doesn't hurt her in the process. If he breaks her heart, he'll have me to answer to.'

'I'm sure you'll always be around to pick up the pieces.'

'Ha!' Alejandro exclaimed. 'If Annalisa will allow me to. My sister's very like you, in that—'

'She's sensible, considerate and as calm as the day is long,' Sadie suggested, tongue-in-cheek.

Alejandro laughed. 'That's not quite how I'd put it,' he said.

'How about you? Tell me something about your family, Sadie.'

Turning his face to the sun, he closed his eyes, as if he sensed how difficult it was for her to relive the past and was giving her space to express her feelings. It did hurt remembering, but he'd opened up, and so should she.

'The day I graduated from catering college, Chef Sorollo and his entire family were sitting in the front row. He's been amazing. I can't tell you how good he's been to me.'

'I know the man, so I know how big his heart is,' Alejandro commented. 'So, now you've started, can you tell me something more?' he prompted when she fell silent.

Sadie drew in a deep, steadying breath. 'I had sent my mother a note, saying how much it would mean to me if she could be at my graduation too…'

'She stayed home,' Alejandro guessed.

Sadie shrugged. 'At least I invited her, but she couldn't make it.'

'Did she write to tell you that?'

'No. She didn't reply.' After all these years that silence still hurt, even though Sadie had always known she was wasting her time trying to enlist her mother's interest. It was just that, somehow, she could never stop hoping.

'That's a deep frown,' Alejandro commented when she had been silent for a while.

'I didn't think you were looking,' she accused lightly.

'Well, I am now.' Squinting against the sun, he shaded his eyes. 'And I'm waiting to hear more. Come on, Sadie,' he coaxed. 'What harm can it do? There's no one here to hear you but me.'

'Then, I'll have to swear you to secrecy.'

'We'll keep it between the two of us,' he promised. 'I won't even make a comment unless you ask me to. How's that?'

She shrugged, but he was right. What did she have to lose? 'I was an accident, apparently.'

'An *accident*?' Alejandro queried. 'Who told you that?'

She smiled a small comic smile. 'My mother.'

'Dios!'

'No, really, it's all right,' Sadie insisted with wry good humour, knowing her mother's rejection had to be so distant from Alejandro's childhood experiences that he was having trouble computing it at all. 'She blamed me for losing her figure—she was a socialite, the type who could never be too thin, or too rich. And that was the cause of the trouble, because they had this great big house and a very glamorous lifestyle, but hardly any money to back it up. And then I came along.'

'A cause for joy, surely?'

'A cause for wailing and gnashing of teeth,' Sadie argued. 'I was just one more problem that was going to cost them money.' She gave a thoughtful sigh. 'It couldn't have been easy for my mother. She never liked me, because I was a drain on the household budget, and when she began to lose her looks, my father started drinking heavily. He used to beat her up when he was intoxicated. She blamed me for that too. We were never close, and I doubt we ever will be. Hey-ho,' she said, forcing a bright note into her voice. 'There are people far worse off than me. Are you still hungry?' she asked as he reached for a hunk of cheese.

'I'm always hungry. Neat change of subject, by the way.'

'I'm learning from a master,' she said.

The expression on Alejandro's face nearly broke her. It was dangerous playing true confessions. They left her vulnerable. Left him vulnerable, Sadie conceded, seeing the shadows behind the compassion in Alejandro's eyes. Maybe they both needed this opportunity to open up a little and let their guards down. If only life could always be so simple, that you could just sit on a riverbank and tell all without fear of being mocked.

'No garlic,' Alejandro said with a lift of his hand, when she offered him some of the pungent bread to go with his cheese.

'I'll eat some too,' she offered.

'Does that mean you're going to kiss me?' he asked with a lift of his brow.

'You wish,' she countered, wishing her cheeks wouldn't always flame red right on cue.

Alejandro angled his stubble-shaded chin. 'Is that you telling me that you have no intention of kissing me today?'

'I've no intention of kissing you any day.'

'You protest too much, I think,' he remarked with a wicked look. 'Maybe it's time for that swim so we can both cool down.'

'Is that water as cold as it looks?' Sadie asked with concern as she glanced at the river.

'Colder,' Alejandro confirmed. 'But if you can swim as well as you ride, it should be a pleasure for you.'

'As in, *if* I survive it will be a pleasure?' Shaking her head, with an amused look she accepted the challenge. 'So, what are we waiting for?'

'For you to strip,' he said flatly.

'After you,' she invited with a challenging smile.

She whizzed her head to one side when he started to work on his belt. 'You could give me some warning.'

'Okay, I'm naked. Is that warning enough?'

Hearing his clothes hit the ground, she tensed, and waited until she heard a splash as he dived in. Only then did she quickly undress down to her modest, serviceable underwear.

The shock of the icy river snatched her breath away, but it also prompted her to swim strongly against the current. Alejandro was right in that she was as confident in the water as she was on horseback, and she soon made good headway towards the opposite bank. The rush of cool, clean glacier melt against her overheated skin was just what she needed, she had decided by the time she found her feet in the shallows.

'This is fantastic,' she confirmed.

'Are you ready to swim back?' Alejandro queried as he shook his thick black hair out of his eyes. 'Or would you prefer to wait until you become an icicle?'

He didn't wait for her answer, which was perhaps as well, Sadie thought as she plunged in after him. The thrill of the race was upon her again, and if they hung around much longer they'd both be frozen solid.

Alejandro's face was a picture when she

swam up alongside him. 'Infuriating woman,' he exclaimed, eyes dancing with laughter, and something far more dangerous, as he helped her up the bank and grabbed his clothes.

Nothing could dull his hunger for Sadie, or his impatience to hold her in his arms. He'd got to know her a bit, and everything he'd learned made him want to know more. Having introduced her to people who lived in these remote areas, and who were generally wary of strangers, he'd seen them welcome Sadie with open arms. They couldn't resist her. She was warm and inclusive, and sharing good food crossed all boundaries. Like music, it brought people together. His mother had been a wonderful cook, and his father a gifted musician. Sadie combined these qualities. Perhaps that was why he was drawn to her. He would be the first to admit that his childhood had been idyllic, while hers had been anything but, which accounted for her wariness, he thought as he watched her clamber out and quickly dress.

When they were dry again and settled on the bank, he thought it the right time to resume their conversation. He was curious about Sadie and wanted to know more.

'So your mother didn't want to know you, but what about your father? Was he not willing to mend fences and attend your graduation?'

'My father cared for me even less than my mother. He blamed his drinking on her, and by extension me, for being the cause of her unhappiness. I've told you that he drank, I should also tell you that his alcoholism led to his early death.'

'It's hard to lose a parent, even, I imagine, if that parent was not the best role model for you. I'm sorry for what you've been through, Sadie. A young girl needs both of her parents.'

'I was sad to lose my father, despite our difficulties, but my mother was relieved and found a younger man within a month of his death.'

'I see,' he said, wondering what other horrors were about to come out. Sadie hadn't finished yet, he suspected.

'Only he came to like me better than my mother, and so she threw me out.'

'Did he touch you?' he asked as fury erupted inside him.

'I left before he had the chance to.'

But goodness knew what had happened before then. 'Do you miss your mother?'

'I don't have anything to miss,' she explained, staring at him intently. 'I'm not like you, Alejandro. I don't have any happy memories to look back on. And I have my own life now...a life that makes me happy.'

'That's good,' he said, though what she said was only partly true, because the scars remained behind her eyes, and that wasn't good.

'I was spoiled,' he admitted wryly, sensing a change of subject was badly needed.

'Tell me,' she encouraged.

For once in his carefully ordered existence, he found he wanted to share. The pain of thinking back was usually better avoided, but as he talked and Sadie listened, he was surprised by how light he felt after confiding in her. She was naturally gregarious with so much love to give. He'd seen that in action when she met his people and they took Sadie to their hearts, and he was seeing it again now.

Was he in danger of becoming involved with this woman? The idea was so unexpected he laughed.

'Well, you've cheered up,' she observed as she rested back on her elbows.

'You amuse me,' he admitted.

'Anyone would think we were getting to know each other,' she observed dryly.

'You're shivering,' he noticed. 'I should have made a fire.' Or there was another way—

She gasped as he brought her into his arms. 'Basic survival tactics,' he insisted. 'Mutual heat...'

CHAPTER NINE

SADIE WAS STILL chilled after her swim, while he was steaming. The urge to be skin-to-skin was overwhelming him, but some instinct warned him to hold off. Her full, tempting lips were only a hair's breadth away, but her eyes were wide and worried.

'Have you never been kissed before?' he suggested as she shivered in his arms.

'I've never been this cold before,' she admitted, teeth chattering uncontrollably. 'No—don't pull away,' she instructed. 'I'm only just beginning to thaw out.'

'Glad I can be of help,' he said as she snuggled closer.

'Any port in a storm,' she teased as he wrapped his arms around her.

'Thanks a lot.'

'Don't mention it,' she murmured, but it

was a relief to hear her smiling. He was glad that she could trust him enough to relax in his arms. It was the biggest sign yet that they were getting to know each other, and that some of the barriers were coming down. 'Better now,' she said, making a token effort to push him away.

He was a man, not a saint, and he brushed her lips with his before pulling away to gauge her reaction.

Challenge darkened her eyes. 'Call that a kiss?'

'No,' he admitted. 'I call this a kiss.'

They came together like an unstoppable force. A starburst of emotion hit Sadie full in the heart as Alejandro drove his mouth down on hers. Blanking all thought, apart from the need to claim him, she felt as if some primal force had taken over from a lifetime of common sense. His tongue probed, her lips parted and pleasure surged. That was all it took for her to demand with everything she'd got that he deepen the kiss even more. No longer a novice, she was learning fast. He kept her marooned on a plateau of pleasure where she was quite happy to stay, making her disappointment all the keener when he let her go.

Cupping her face, he stared fiercely into her eyes. 'I don't know what happened to you in the past, but I do know this is now, and I want you.'

It was such a primal thing for him to say she was excited beyond reason. But then her sensible side took over. The fire in Alejandro's eyes might dare her to believe him, but did he want her for a few hours, for a few days, or for eternity, and what did she have to say about those options?

'I never say anything I don't mean,' he said as he traced her kiss-swollen lips with his forefinger.

'And I never agree to anything unless I'm certain,' she countered, pulling back.

'Then, this might turn out to be a very long seduction indeed.'

'A seduction?' she queried.

Thinking better of where this was heading, she put some more distance between them. She might be drawn to Alejandro, but she had no intention of setting herself up for heart-break. Confident in every other area of her life, she knew nothing about happy relationships between a man and a woman, and where they were concerned she always shied away.

'Caution rules you,' Alejandro observed in a lazy growl, not in the least bit fazed, 'and that's something I intend to change.'

Could anyone? she wondered.

She should have remembered how experienced he was, and when he kissed her again, and kept on kissing her gently and persuasively, she felt so safe, though at the back of her mind there remained the nagging thought that her heart was in danger. But his drugging kisses made her want him even more, and the clothes she'd so quickly tugged on were slowly being peeled off again.

'I want you.'

The wicked murmur in her ear echoed Sadie's own thoughts. She guessed Alejandro didn't need an answer when he could feel how taut with anticipation she was, and see how hunger was blazing from her eyes. Her breasts ached, and her nipples were thrusting imperatively against his chest. Every atom in her body craved him, and he knew this. The faint smile on his hard mouth had the power to make her forget everything, and his kisses to her neck, her cheeks, her eyes and her lips, while his hands worked a special brand of magic on her body, made the outcome certain.

Until he pulled back.

'What did I do?' She stared up, uncomprehending. 'If this is a joke—'

'No joke,' he said. 'Just not here and not yet.'

He was content to bring her to the point of surrender, only to draw back? Now, she was mad. 'You're a tease,' she said, pushing him away. 'I thought we were starting to trust each other, but it seems that I'm guilty of being naive again.'

'Not naive,' he argued. 'Inexperienced.'

'Stupid,' she countered, springing up.

'We should return to camp,' he said, unconcerned. 'Are you coming, or are you staying there?' he asked as he began to tack up their horses.

'Neither,' Sadie gritted out as she went to mount her horse.

* * *

Alejandro was confident he had made the right decision, though all the ease between them had disappeared. They rode straight back to camp without a single word of conversation. Sadie must regret kissing him and letting her guard down, and now she wasn't sure how to come back from it. Don't even try, he thought. As the supreme master of checks and control, even he knew that sometimes a change of mind was for the best.

Self-restraint was a self-imposed discipline, and one he'd put in place ten years ago on the day his parents were killed, when both Annalisa and the Dukedom of Alegon became his responsibility. Before that date, he had enjoyed all the trappings of wealth and success, but with that one shattering revelation, everything changed for ever. Surprising himself, he hadn't missed his hedonistic lifestyle for a single moment, until now, when the urge to bed Sadie was like a madness raging inside him. Anyone who said delay was the servant of pleasure had no idea what it was like to be tortured like this, but if he was going to seduce her, it wouldn't be on a frozen riverbank, but in comfort where he could take his time.

When they reached camp, it was packed with people. Fiesta was in the air, and Marissa was waiting for Sadie. 'Dance with me!' she begged, practically jumping up and down.

'I will,' Sadie promised with that soft, genuine smile she kept for her friends, 'but I have to rub my horse down first.' Dismounting, she added, 'And I need to freshen up and change.'

'Have you been swimming?' Marissa asked. 'Alejandro, you haven't!' His sister turned to face him. 'I thought swimming in that freezing river was a torture you kept for yourself. You surely haven't inflicted it on Sadie? You have,' she scolded as he sprang to the ground. 'Anyway, everyone's going to be dancing tonight, and you're going to be with us,' she told Sadie. 'And, don't worry, I'll protect you from my crazy brother. You certainly don't need *him* to guide your steps.'

'Too right,' Sadie agreed with a sharp look at him. 'Horse comfort comes first, and then I'll freshen up and see you back here in half an hour.'

'Don't be any longer, or you'll miss the fun,' Marissa insisted, sharing a brilliant smile with Sadie, and a scowl for him.

As soon as Sadie was out of earshot, Marissa turned to him. 'Alejandro?' Her tone was accusing. 'What on earth have you been up to now?'

'What's your problem?' he grunted, not in the best of moods.

'You,' Marissa said bluntly. 'You're my problem. I really like Sadie, and if you hurt her, I'll kill you.'

'That's a bit dramatic, isn't it?' he commented, raising a brow. 'And you'd have to catch me first,' he added, teasing his sister as he always had, but this time Marissa refused to be amused.

'This isn't a joke, Alejandro,' she assured him. 'I know how you can switch the charm on and off, and, as your sister, I'm not going to hold back.'

'You never have before,' he commented dryly.

'She likes you,' Marissa said, narrowing her eyes as she stared across the camp at Sadie, who was just entering the shower block. 'Goodness knows why, but there we are.'

Thumbing his jaw, he made no comment.

Huffing with impatience, Marissa glared into his eyes. 'She could be good for you, Alejandro—if you'd let her be. She could be the best thing that ever happened to you. She might even manage to save you from yourself.'

'On what evidence?' he queried.

'On the evidence of my own eyes, and the reaction of our people, or does their judgement count for nothing with you these days? She's kind, and she's funny—'

'Funny?' he interrupted. 'You must see a different side to Sadie.'

'Do you give her chance?' Marissa countered. 'Beneath those chef's whites is a warm, tender, honest woman, and you could do with some light-heartedness in your life.'

'Keep out of it,' he warned quietly. 'This has nothing to do with you.'

'Apart from the fact that I refuse to stand back and let you mess this up, do you mean?' his sister demanded with a fierce stare.

'I'm not going to argue with you,' he said.

'Because you know I'm right,' she insisted. 'We both know that women like Sadie Montgomery don't grow on trees. Fate has thrown her in your path, but fate won't keep her there. It's up to you to do that.'

His expression said, *blah-de-blah-de-blah*, but as he walked away he had a feeling Marissa could be right.

Sadie had fantasised about Alejandro kissing her, but the reality had so far exceeded her wildest dreams. She was still buzzing with excitement, and fury with herself that she'd let things go so far, only for Alejandro to pull back.

Give yourself a break, Sadie reasoned as she strode across camp towards Marissa's caravan. Fantasies featuring Alejandro were excusable. He was hot as hell and had a particular brand of blistering sensuality that no one could ignore, and one kiss wasn't the end of the world.

One kiss?

Okay, so several kisses.

But not enough kisses?

Thankfully, the door to Marissa's caravan

was open to welcome Sadie back, so she could put all thoughts of kisses out of her mind. Well, that was the theory, anyway. But she did smile again, and broadly, to see her dancing clothes laid out on the bed. It was good to be made to feel so welcome, and as the two women hugged Sadie knew that she had made another valued friend in Marissa. Chef Sorollo was right in saying she should get out and about more. There were a lot of nice people in the world, if she only took the trouble to find them.

'Stand still,' Marissa insisted as she made the final tweaks to Sadie's appearance. 'You're like a cat on a hot tin roof. The effect of my brother, I suppose.'

'No,' Sadie protested, though her aroused body called her a liar. 'I just can't wait to get up on that stage and learn to dance.'

'And if he's watching you?'

Sadie's pulse raced at the thought. 'I can't imagine your brother would be interested in watching me, when there are bound to be so many experts on the stage.'

As Marissa hummed, Sadie promised herself she wouldn't get carried away emotionally where the Gypsy King was concerned. She was still glad she'd come to the mountains, because it had shown her a new way of life, but when they left here Sadie and Alejandro would resume their normal lives.

'The dancing is about to begin,' Marissa warned. 'We should leave now…'

The moment she mounted the stage, the first person Sadie looked for was Alejandro. *I'm a lost cause*, she concluded as she stumbled through the steps of the first dance.

'Concentrate,' Marissa insisted when Sadie almost lost her balance. 'Forget *him* and listen to the music. Allow the rhythm and the melody to dictate your moves…and don't be afraid to toss your hair and use your body, as well as your eyes. Flamenco is all about passion. The dance isn't just a series of moves. It expresses life and emotion in all its richness.'

'If I could get everything to work in sync, I might be able to follow your advice,' Sadie admitted, laughing.

But eventually something did happen. There were so many people on the stage she didn't feel as exposed as she had expected, and whatever Alejandro might think of her amateurish attempt to copy the other dancers, he couldn't knock her for lack of enthusiasm. Like everything else she did, she tried her hardest, and it wasn't an impossible task when the click of castanets drove her feet to follow the rhythm, and the rise and fall of the melody tugged at her heartstrings. Finally, she concluded that, whether Alejandro approved of her efforts or not, she was here, and she was going to nail this.

When the musicians took a break, Marissa had a chance to question Sadie about her day with Alejandro. It only occurred to Sadie then that he maddened her, thrilled her and excited her like no one else. And that maybe…just maybe, she was falling in love with him. But her feelings were like a tender shoot that could so easily be trampled. And anyway, Alejandro's feelings for her were as clear as mud.

'It was very nice,' she said carefully. 'I sourced some really good recipes.'

'Very nice?' Marissa echoed. 'You spend the

day with Alejandro and expect me to believe you did nothing more than collect recipes?'

'Some really good ones,' Sadie insisted, widening her eyes.

'I can see I'm not going to get anything from you,' Marissa complained as she pulled a comic face.

'That's right, you're not,' Sadie agreed with a grin, 'but only because there's nothing to find out.'

'So, why are you staring at my brother?' Marissa demanded as the band started up again.

'I'm not staring.' She was evaluating, Sadie reasoned, watching as Alejandro chatted to the people around him. He was such a different man in the mountains, approachable and affable. By contrast, in Madrid he seemed restless and remote. Always another deal to close, she supposed.

'Concentrate,' Marissa scolded.

Her friend was trying hard to hide a grin, Sadie noticed. 'There's nothing between me and your brother.'

'So, it should be easy to forget he's watching you.'

'He's watching me?' Sadie sounded alarmed, which made Marissa laugh.

'You have to forget everything except the dance,' she said. 'Even my brother.'

Which was easier said than done when Sadie's frowning gaze landed on Alejandro's swarthy face.

'Dance,' Marissa commanded.

Breaking eye contact with Alejandro with relief, Sadie threw all her pent-up feelings into the dance.

'Olé!'

The deep, cynical voice that sounded behind her could only belong to one man. *'Olé,* yourself,' she said, turning to face him. 'Are you determined to throw me off balance?'

'I'm determined to dance with you,' he said, and, swinging her into his arms, he did just that.

'It's polite to ask first,' she informed him, fighting off the sense that her body was most definitely winning this clash, and that her sensible mind wasn't required on the battlefield.

'Polite?' Alejandro queried in amusement. Locking his arm around her waist, he brought her so close they shared the same breath, the same air.

'If this is your idea of teasing me again...' Sadie protested.

'Would you like me to tease you again?' he suggested.

Firming her jaw, she refused to answer, and turned her face away to avoid the heat in his eyes. She'd seen enough of that firm, smiling, ridiculously sexy mouth, and if dance was a prelude to sex, she'd have none of it.

Oh, for goodness' sake! her inner voice protested. *Do you feel safe and protected?*

Yes.

Will you miss Alejandro when you both return to Madrid and normal life is resumed?

Yes again.

So, why not enjoy the moment? If you play it safe all your life you'll never have any memories to enjoy.

'You're a good dancer as well as a good rider and swimmer,' he commented. 'Do you have any other skills I should know about?'

'I can cook.'

He laughed. 'You certainly can, but you also have a great sense of rhythm.'

'It must be kneading all that dough,' she snapped.

Hearing how angry she sounded, she laughed at the absurdity of being at daggers drawn with Alejandro because he'd kissed her and she'd enjoyed it.

He laughed too, which was the signal for them both to relax. How could she not enjoy this, when she was dancing with the most incredible man, who, with his strong, proud face and incredible body—a body that she might have taken a small peek at on the riverbank, 'small peek' being the only small thing about that encounter, cold water having absolutely no effect on him—would have Michelangelo lunging for his chisel? After all, they were only dancing.

Only dancing?

Yes. Where was the harm in that?

Dancing so close that her body was already pulsing with pleasure was dangerous, but when one tune segued seamlessly into the next and she didn't make the smallest attempt to pull away, the music cast its spell, urging her to forget caution and consider the possibility of one night in Alejandro's arms. It could do no harm and might even help to get rid of her insecurities. During their many conversations, Marissa had told her that Alejandro's parents had instilled in him a deep respect for women, so she'd be safe, and what better teacher could she have?

Would she be safe? It wasn't Alejandro she had to worry about, but her all too vulnerable heart.

'Spend the night with me.'

She glanced up, wondering if she'd misheard him.

'Spend the night with me,' he repeated.

The musicians had started to play a slow, wistful tune that suggested absence and longing, and a sudden rush of emotion made all the things she knew she should say stall on her lips.

Taking her silence as agreement, Alejandro led the way off the stage, and they walked across the camp together, but not towards Marissa's caravan. He stopped outside another heavily decorated dwelling, which was hidden deep in a leafy glade.

'Welcome to my mountain retreat,' he said, and, reaching past her, he opened the door on the shadowy interior. 'This is the place I consider to be my true mountain home,' he explained as she walked up the steps.

'This is where you were born,' she guessed, and where he returned to reboot and to recover from the pressure of the city, Sadie suspected as Alejandro shut the door behind them, enclosing them in the comforting warmth.

Lit only by moonlight, it was a deeply romantic space. Comfortably furnished, the traditional caravan was heavily shaded, with a comfortable settle and a large double bed. It was a magical hideaway in the forest, Sadie thought as her heart started racing at the sight of Alejandro leaning back against the door. How could he look so sexy? Even the shadows loved him, throwing his cheekbones into sharp relief and making his eyes gleam in the darkness.

Sexual tension soared between them, until,

as if all the barriers had suddenly come tumbling down, he reached out and she sprang into his arms.

CHAPTER TEN

THERE WAS NO caution and no acknowledgement from Sadie that she was a virgin with no experience of men. She only knew what she wanted and needed, and that was Alejandro. Like two tigers mating they ripped at each other's clothes. Two equals meeting, and demanding everything from each other, meant skin scorched against skin, as if a tornado had torn through the confined space. Cushions and throws hit the floor. Personal belongings went flying, until, finally, breathlessly, she was naked and so was he.

When Alejandro brought her into his arms this time, she responded by reaching up to weave her fingers through his thick, wavy hair to keep him close. There was no blushing, no shame, no surprise at feeling his very masculine contours thrusting against her softer, yielding body. There was only eagerness to claim her mate, and to be claimed. No thought of consequences crossed her mind.

Alejandro's kisses were seductive and addictive, and as he pressed her down on the bed the helpful night threw a thick black blanket of privacy around them, making it seem to Sadie that they were the only two people in the world. Her senses were heightened to an incredible degree, so that each touch and kiss threatened to tip her over the edge into a pleasure she couldn't even imagine. Their breathing, her heartbeat and his, and the fact that Alejandro's brutally masculine body was poised above hers with such restraint, only made her want him more. He smelled so good, so warm and masculine, musky and clean, and he tasted minty and fresh. But it was his cherishing touch that moved her almost to tears. There was something different about him that she couldn't quite pinpoint. Then she realised it was tenderness, which was the last thing she had expected from him, and it made emotion surge inside her.

'You're a virgin.'

SUSAN STEPHENS

His words shocked her. They hung in the air between them like an accusation, shattering the spell and bringing harsh reality into the world of passion. 'How can you tell?' she asked defensively. 'Did I do something wrong?'

'You should have told me,' he said, drawing back.

'So, now you know.'

'I suspected,' he said, 'but now I'm certain.'

'And...?'

'And now you have to be doubly sure that this is what you want,' he said.

'I am sure. I've never wanted anything more,' Sadie admitted. 'But if you don't want—'

Alejandro answered this, as well as her self-doubt, with a kiss so lingering and gentle he moved her to tears. She had never felt a touch like his, or received such devoted attention before. She'd never believed in fate bringing people together. Sheer hard work, and the ability to be flexible, had seen her through. There had never been any room in her life for romance, but it seemed that tonight fate had the last laugh.

'Slow down,' he said as she reached for him.

'I don't want to slow down.' She'd waited a lifetime to experience closeness and had no intention of wasting a single second of the night. She didn't need reminding that her reality lay in Madrid, and that this was a fantasy that probably wouldn't travel as well as the precious recipes she'd collected in the mountains.

Gasping with pleasure at the touch of his hands, she arched her naked back, inviting more of his kisses. He didn't keep her waiting...for anything.

Suckling her nipples while she writhed beneath him, he sank his face deep and rasped his stubble very lightly against her breasts. 'I love your body.'

She answered by winding her legs around him. 'And I love yours, so don't stop this time. Don't ever stop,' she instructed in a whisper as he paused to tease.

Working her hips urgently, she hunted for more contact. 'Oh, please... I need this.'

'It's your first time,' he reminded her as he raised himself high on his fists, and then he kissed her into silence, telling her she was beautiful as he moved down the bed.

He lavished kisses and caresses everywhere but where she needed him most, heating her with his breath in a way that sent her arousal soaring. She was so pale against his dark skin in the moonlight, but the gulf between them went a lot deeper than that, Sadie thought as she moved restlessly on the bed. Here in the unlikely setting of a Romani caravan hidden away in the mountains, she was Sadie and he was Alejandro, and it was as simple as that, but when they returned to Madrid—

'Stop,' he said, breaking into her thoughts. 'You're tensing, and I know that's because you're thinking about things that might never happen and if I'm the cause of that, I'll stop.'

'So, it doesn't matter that I'm a chef and you're a—?'

'Irrelevant,' he stated flatly, 'and I don't want to hear that ever again. There is no status in the mountains, and none between you and me, wherever we might be. Your responsibilities while you're here extend only as far as the right to enjoy yourself, and to gain whatever knowledge you think appropriate to your work.'

'Like this?' she queried, smiling.

Alejandro laughed and the tension between them dissolved, along with Sadie's doubts. Kisses, awareness and arousal filled her world as Alejandro pleasured her with all the skill she had expected. Trembling with urgency beneath him, she held her breath as he brought her to the edge and kept her there. Cupping her buttocks with one hand, he increased his attention with the other hand until control became impossible. With a scream she let go and was still in the throes of unimaginable pleasure when he spread her legs wide and knelt between them.

Taking her slowly and carefully with the lightest shallow thrust, he pulled back before repeating the action several times, on each occasion moving a little deeper, until at last he had taken possession of her body. A brief moment of discomfort was easily eclipsed by the enormity of the pleasure.

'I'll never get enough of you,' he said as she groaned with surprised delight and approval.

Reaching up, she brought him close for more kisses, and it was a long time later, when she was snuggled safe in his arms, that she sighed with contentment and drifted off to sleep. Some time in the night she woke up, and immediately turned to look for Alejandro. 'You're not asleep,' she whispered with concern.

'I'm watching over you,' he said.

'More dark angel than guardian angel,' she remarked as she smiled and ran a fingertip down the side of his stubble-blackened jaw.

'I wouldn't argue with that,' he growled as he caught her finger in his mouth. His suckling it forced her to acknowledge the sweet, demanding pulses of her body.

'More?' Alejandro suggested as she moved restlessly on the bed.

'Please...'

He smiled against her mouth. 'Ride me,' he whispered.

He helped her with his hands guiding her buttocks, but as the need inside her grew she didn't need him, and worked furiously to bring them both the release they craved. It was an explosion of passion that rocked the caravan, as well as Sadie, to her foundations. The starburst of pleasure was seemingly endless, and with each pleasure wave she felt closer and closer to Alejandro. When she was finally quiet again, she sank on top of him, gasping for breath.

'Better now?' he murmured as he stroked her hair to soothe her down. Wrapping her in his arms, he brought her beneath him to drop kisses on her mouth that tempted her to believe this was for ever.

'What?' he probed when she stared off into the middle distance.

'You. Me. Everything,' she said.

Alejandro moved to lie beside her so they could look at each other in the darkness. 'Haven't I reassured you?' he asked. 'Is the past still haunting you? And if it is, what can I do to help?'

Sadie laughed softly. 'Where do I start?'

'By being proud of the fact that whatever happened in the past, you came through and made a successful life for yourself. That should be your starting point,' Alejandro insisted.

'I do love my work,' she admitted, thinking about the busy kitchen in Madrid. 'I'll never be able to thank Chef Sorollo enough for giving me that first chance.'

'I imagine he's glad he found you,' Alejandro observed. 'So, that's not the problem. It goes back a lot further than that. Can you talk about it?'

'It's not easy.'

'I didn't expect it to be,' he assured her in a wry tone that matched her thinking.

Heaving in a breath, she began. 'When my father died, I hoped that my mother would feel safe at last, and we could be reconciled and face the future together, but that wasn't to be. Nothing changed about her attitude towards me when my father died. Nothing at all.'

'That's hard for me to understand,' Alejandro admitted.

'Because you were raised surrounded by love and warmth.'

'Which I took for granted.'

'But you're aware of it, and it made you confident and strong.'

'You're confident and strong,' he argued.

'In some ways, yes,' Sadie agreed.

'Why not all ways?' Alejandro queried, pulling his head back to stare into her eyes. 'You built your own sturdy foundations, while mine were built for me, so who's the stronger person now?'

She was silent for a while, and then she admitted with a crooked smile, 'I guess we're both strong.'

'Exactly,' Alejandro agreed, and from tender amusement his expression darkened to one she recognised, and, reaching for each other, they made love again.

She must have slept for hours. It was chilly when she woke up…and no wonder…she was alone and naked, and there was no sign of Alejandro. Panic scorched through her veins. Thinking back to the previous night should have eased her fears, consisting as it had of passion, fun and tenderness. *But where was he?* The shower block, maybe?

Her body was still throbbing with pleasure and the memory of Alejandro's touch as she tossed the bedclothes into some sort of order and got dressed.

He wasn't in the shower block, so perhaps he had taken his horse for an early ride. He had to be somewhere nearby. He wouldn't just leave. Making love had brought them so close that disappearing without a word was surely impossible?

She'd never experienced anything like it before, Sadie mused as she walked through the camp. Far from the discomfort she'd been expecting for her first time, Alejandro had made it perfect. But it was more than physical pleasure that she'd taken from last night. Bodies shared, eyes connecting, spirits soaring, and the humour! She hadn't expected that. And the more they'd laughed, the wilder they'd become. Then later, when he'd made love to her slowly and so very thoroughly, she'd felt complete. She wasn't alone anymore. There *was* magic in the mountains, Sadie concluded as she spun around, propelled by sheer joy. She had absolutely no doubt of that now.

Half an hour later, she wasn't so sure. Having searched every inch of the camp, she was starting to worry, and when she asked one of the dancers, the woman said bluntly, 'He's gone.'

Air gushed from Sadie's lungs. 'Gone? Gone where? Gone riding, do you mean?' she asked tensely.

'No.'

Sadie's heart clenched tight as the woman gazed up at the sky. When she followed that gaze, she saw the sleek black helicopter on the point of disappearing behind a cloud.

'El Duque has left us to attend to his responsibilities in the city,' the woman explained, confirming Sadie's worst fears. She'd been deserted *again*.

And so ends the fairy tale, she thought, biting back tears as she faced the reality of Alejandro's leaving her. Thanking the woman, she walked away, heading for the shower block. She stood beneath the water for a long time until she was calm again, and knew exactly what she had to do. After towelling down, she dressed and headed for Marissa's caravan, where she would pack and change into suitable clothes for the journey. She wouldn't be returning to Madrid with her tail between her legs. This was an opportunity to seize back control of her life and put the past in its proper context.

Leaving Sadie was the hardest thing he had ever had to do, and he hated himself for having to do it so abruptly. He could only hope she'd read the note he'd left on the bed, and understood that this trip was unavoidable. Protecting Sadie from more hurt was paramount. That, and a growing business crisis in Madrid, meant he had no option but to call for one of his company helicopters to collect him right away. Waking Sadie, who had been sleeping so peacefully, would serve no purpose, other than to worry her.

Would she wait? Would she trust him? Would she trust him enough?

For once in his charmed existence, he couldn't be sure, but neither could he be in two places at once, and with Sadie's welfare at the forefront of his mind, as well as the livelihoods of those families who depended on him, he had no choice but to return at once.

Trying to raise Sadie on the phone to make sure she'd got his note proved fruitless. For some reason, she wasn't picking up. If she'd missed the note, he could only imagine how she was feeling. Placing a call to Marissa, and then to Maria at his house in the mountains as his helicopter soared high above the land, proved equally frustrating. Why was no one answering? Sadie had been through enough without him adding to her distress.

Without the love and guidance of Chef Sorollo, Sadie could have been lost down the cracks like so many other unwanted children.

Alejandro had always been a firm believer in confronting demons before they had chance to gain a hold, but Sadie had been all alone up to the point where she met Chef Sorollo and had chosen to avoid them by throwing herself into work. If she couldn't come to terms with the fact that her mother didn't want her, she would never leave the nightmare behind. His mission was to help her to do that, and as soon as he'd dealt with the crisis in Madrid, that was exactly what he would do.

* * *

The mountains had certainly changed everything for her, Sadie thought as she shared a tearful goodbye with Marissa. She had made some wonderful friends, and the clean mountain air had cleared her mind as well as her lungs, making things she'd avoided for far too long seem suddenly like urgent matters to deal with.

Marissa insisted on driving her to the airport in a battered old Jeep that had seen better days.

'You should ask Alejandro to buy you a new one,' Sadie joked as the gears ground a noisy complaint.

'Why should I?' Marissa patted the steering wheel fondly. 'This old girl might have caused me some trouble, but she hasn't got the better of me yet.'

Sadie had one wobbly moment when they drove past Castillo Fuego, but, firming her resolve, she silently thanked Alejandro for giving her the opportunity to learn so much about the wonderful mountain community.

'As soon as the equipment is delivered, I'll

be back to check everything is working as it should be, and that Maria is happy with her new kitchen,' she promised.

'And Alejandro?' Marissa probed gently.

'If he's here I'll see him, I guess. Ours is a professional relationship,' she said, frowning as if to convince herself.

Marissa's mouth firmed, as if she had to stop herself saying something she might regret, and they drove the rest of the way to the airport in silence. That was almost a relief for Sadie. Alejandro's shock departure hurt too much for her to talk about it. It brought back all those memories of being rejected as a child, and that was something she most certainly wanted to forget.

CHAPTER ELEVEN

HE WAS SEATED at a table in El Gato Feroz, waiting for his bill after a most delicious meal. 'I would like to compliment the chef,' he told the waitress, knowing that chef was Sadie, thanks to inside information from Chef Sorollo.

'I'm sure she'll be thrilled, Don Alegon,' the waitress, a woman new to the restaurant, who knew nothing of the history between him and Sadie, told him.

Thrilled? He wasn't so sure about that. He wasn't even sure Sadie would come out to see him.

But she did.

'Don Alegon,' she said politely.

Even dressed in stark chef's whites, she looked more beautiful to him than any of the elegant society women in the restaurant. 'That was a wonderful meal. I can't eat better any-where in the world than here.'

'Cut the flannel,' she murmured discreetly. 'It isn't necessary and I don't appreciate it. Thank you, Don Alegon,' she added in a louder voice. 'It's a great honour for the team to have you eat here.'

'I'm sure it is,' he murmured with an ironic smile. 'I'll pick you up at midnight,' he added so only she could hear. 'Don't keep me wait-ing.' Pushing his chair back, he stood, and strode out of the restaurant without a back-ward glance. There was no point being soft with a strong woman like Sadie. She'd have no respect if he treated her with kid gloves. They had long passed the point of dancing around each other. The gloves were off. It was time for stark home truths. Either that, or move on, and he had no intention of walking out on Sadie.

He drove back later that evening in a vehi-cle that matched his need for speed. Sadie, dressed in jeans and a casual jacket with the collar turned up, walked out of the back door of the restaurant as he pulled up. Walking over, she climbed in. After exchanging the usual civilities, they drove in silence to his house in Madrid. The air in the enclosed cabin of the low-slung muscle machine was full of pent-up tension. He guessed they both had a lot to say.

When they arrived, he showed her into his study and invited her to sit down.

'I prefer to stand, thank you,' she told him in a clipped tone.

Unfazed, he queried, 'Don't you ever answer your phone?'

'Yes, but I'm lucky enough to be able to choose who I speak to.'

'Like my sisters,' he commented without emotion.

Her jaw seemed to set just that little bit harder, but she made no reply.

'Do I deduce from your silence that you and my sisters are united in your disapproval of me?'

'Think what you like,' she said. 'You walk out on me without a word? Couldn't you have woken me before you left? No,' she said, answering her own question. 'The mighty Duke isn't used to answering to anyone. He just makes a decision and walks away, without considering how that might affect anyone else.'

'Will you give me chance to explain?' When she said nothing, he told her what had happened. 'There was a crisis at one of my factories. I take a hands-on approach, and I needed to be there in person to make sure everything was smoothed out to my employees' satisfaction. I left you a note with my explanation.'

'As for this note you left, I didn't see anything before I left.'

'Because you were too angry, and in too much of a hurry to get away?' he suggested. When she didn't answer, he assured her, 'I left that note on the bed where I was certain you would see it. I tried to call you dozens of times, but you obviously didn't want to speak to me, and neither did my sisters.'

Sadie had felt excluded and forgotten after putting the ultimate trust in him, he guessed from her angry silence. She must think he'd simply taken what he wanted, and then left her. Misunderstandings were deadly, and because of Sadie's past, even more so.

'I'm not part of your history,' he bit out. 'Let

go of what happened all those years ago. Don't let it crush you.'

'Don't allow you to crush me, don't you mean? Any more instructions?' she snapped, eyes blazing with doubt and mistrust when he remained silent for a while.

'Yes,' he said when she was calmer. 'Don't let the past influence your belief in the future. Live in the here and now.'

'Like you?' She glanced around. 'Are you so happy? You've told me what a wonderful family home you had, and how your childhood was idyllic, yet all you have achieved is a portfolio of fabulous properties across the world. You don't have a single place to call home.'

'My caravan in the mountains is my home,' he reminded her, adding, 'Sadie, I wouldn't hurt you for the world. We both have obstacles to overcome. I know that.'

With a shrug, she shook her head. 'I still find it rather hard to believe that, with all your resources, you couldn't get hold of me to explain.'

'There are some things I prefer to keep private,' he assured her, 'and I wanted to see you face-to-face.'

'Well, you've got your wish, so now what?'

Her fury had brought them dangerously close. Tension was at an all-time high. 'Don't touch me,' she warned with the fiercest of looks.

'Why not? Are you afraid of how that might make you feel?'

Catching hold of her wrist as she went to push him away brought their faces close. She took over, and with a growl of fury she laced her other hand through his hair, and, dragging him close, she kissed him.

'That's what it felt like when you left,' she said as she pushed him away. 'You can't just walk back into my life when it suits you, and pick up where you left off.'

'Yes, I can,' he argued as he pulled her back to him.

'Don't do that,' she warned as he teased her lips with his tongue.

'Why? Don't you like it? Or do you like it too much?'

With a groan she pulled him back for more

kisses. One thing led to another, until neither of them could wait. Slipping his hand between her legs, he felt her readiness. 'Yes?' he ground out.

Sadie's answer was to work on his belt, and she sloughed off his jeans faster than he could undress her. They were on the rug before he had chance to rip off his top. Parting her legs, he moved between them. She wrapped them around his waist.

There was no foreplay. None required. He took her fast and deep as she arced towards him, and they worked furiously towards the inevitable release.

It was as if the need to stake their claim could only be achieved with more pleasure than either of them had ever known before, and when he suggested moving somewhere more comfortable during a brief, breath-snatching lull, she informed him that he wasn't going anywhere and neither was she, which she went on to prove most convincingly by drawing him back into the dark, insatiable world of carnal hunger.

It was dawn when they finally lay quietly

side by side, and he turned to look at Sadie to find her eyes closed. Was she asleep, or was she just hiding her thoughts from him? He didn't have to wait long to find out. Standing up, she grabbed her clothes and dressed.

'Where are you going?' he asked.

'To shower in one of your many state-of-the-art bathrooms, and then back to work, of course.'

He had expected to spend the day together and frowned. 'Won't you stay for breakfast, at least?'

'I'm busy. I've got work to do, as I'm sure you do,' she told him briskly.

'Sadie—'

'Goodbye, Alejandro, and thank you for the advice. I'm getting the hang of this living-in-the-moment business, and maybe it's enough for me. Time will tell,' she added lightly as she left the room.

Well and truly hoisted by his own petard, Alejandro swore viciously as he sprang to his feet. What maddened him the most, he decided as he tugged on his clothes, was that every twist and turn with Sadie only made him want her more. And the surprises didn't end there. When he rang the restaurant to ask her what the hell was going on, a receptionist who knew nothing about their relationship said Chef Sadie was away sourcing equipment for some big design job she was handling in the mountains, and would be returning to the Sierra Nevada before she came back to Madrid.

He'd been blindsided by a woman every bit as good as he was at being evasive when it suited her. With an ironic laugh, he conceded Sadie hadn't told him where her work would take her next.

Work could really screw up his personal life, and it had been almost a month since he'd spoken to Sadie. In that time she'd worked miracles apparently, and his staff were queuing up to sing her praises. Distance might make the heart grow fonder, but it had upped his frustration to an unsustainable level. His sister was next in line to bear the brunt of his bad temper.

'So, you're speaking to me now,' he snapped as he flew from Madrid to the mountains.

'Only to warn you not to get in Sadie's way.

She's doing an amazing job on the kitchen, according to Maria.'

Forced to listen to how thrilled everyone was, and how everything was running smoothly thanks to Sadie, he tapped his foot impatiently. But at least he knew for certain where she was. 'Tell her to remain where she is until I arrive. She's not taking my calls, for some reason.'

'I can't imagine why,' Annalisa retorted sarcastically. 'And I can't tell her what to do. Is Sadie supposed to second-guess how long you're going to be away? Her work is just as important to her as yours is to you.' There was a silence and then his sister added, 'What have you done, Alejandro? What have you said to her? Sadie must have a good reason not to speak to you.'

'I need her to be there for the annual flamenco party,' he said, ignoring this. 'Sadie should know the new kitchen better than anyone, and her food is second to none.'

'You want her to cook for you now?' Annalisa demanded with incredulity. 'I can't believe your cheek. Lucky for you, I believe she's already discussed this with Chef Sorollo, and plans to organise and personally supervise the event.'

'Bueno,' he grunted.

'Don't you dare upset her when you arrive,' Annalisa warned.

'As if I would,' he gritted out softly.

Sadie was just as likely to upset him. So far she'd made a pretty good job of it—walking out on him, and then avoiding his calls. But with his business issues wrapped up in Madrid, he was hot on her trail. There was just one frustrating delay ahead of him, when he visited the flamenco camp to make sure everyone was happy with the arrangements he'd made for their performance at his party. It was the social event of the year in the area and would garner a great deal of publicity for the professional dancers. Whatever he could do to showcase their talent, he would do.

He was flying in the small jet he used to criss-cross the world, but once he landed, he would transfer to a helicopter to make his travels in the mountains easier and faster. Sadie had inflamed his senses beyond endurance.

All he could think of was being near her again—to make love with her, to have her challenge him, and to passionately make up.

Perhaps even more than that, he mused as he lowered the landing gear, he looked forward to basking in the warm ambience she created, proving her right, he supposed, when she referred to his vast property empire as impressive, but lacking a home. Each of his residences was full of expensive props, programmed to work in exactly the same way, so there were no surprises when he arrived. Nothing was allowed to interfere with his seamless existence. How he'd feel about a new kitchen remained to be seen, though he doubted he'd visit the facility more than a couple of times. The greater problem would be that anything Sadie had designed would remind him of her.

CHAPTER TWELVE

PREGNANT!

Sadie stared at the thin blue line in disbelief. Okay, she reasoned when she finally caught her breath. It was a few weeks since she'd seen Alejandro, and they'd certainly worked hard enough at shortening the odds.

Having her suspicions in Madrid, she had dashed to the pharmacy to pick up some tests shortly before boarding the flight for the mountains. She had just completed the last of them in her luxurious suite of rooms at Alejandro's mountain mansion, which was about as conducive to homey, cosy, motherly thoughts as a rather upmarket hotel room. She had lined up five tests on the porcelain sink, each showing a positive result. There was no room for doubt. She was pregnant! Ecstatic didn't go far enough to describe her feelings. A family of her own was all she had ever dreamed of, though she did have some reservations, since pregnancy, babies and motherhood were all new to her. Her biggest concern was that she had what it took to be a good mother. Without a pattern to follow, she could only do her best. She would, Sadie determined as a fresh rush of excitement swooped over her. Babies didn't come with an instruction manual, so she would be starting from scratch like every other new mother.

Work had kept her busy, and it was only when she'd felt sick one morning that she had decided to check, and now she knew for sure she had to tell Alejandro. She hoped she got the chance before things went too much further. She was in the middle of arranging a party for him, while he was visiting the flamenco camp with no definite time or date set for his arrival. All she knew was that he would arrive in time for the party.

Standing in front of the mirror in the marble-clad bathroom, she took a deep breath to steady herself, and then sluiced her face in cold water before patting it dry and applying enough make-up to hide the pallor in her cheeks. For the first time in years, she missed having a mother to confide in. Pregnancy came with so many hopes and fears, but one thing was certain: she would fight for her child with everything she'd got.

And Alejandro? What would his reaction be?

She'd find out soon enough. Tomorrow the dark and dangerously alluring Duque de Alegon would be holding his annual flamenco party for the great and good, here at his fabulous mountain retreat.

The following day, Sadie was flooded with mixed emotions. And knowing Alejandro was close by made her heart go crazy. She couldn't wait to tell him her news and was impatient to gauge his reaction. If he turned his back, she was quite capable of going it alone. If he wanted to be part of everything, she had to handle him so he didn't march in and take over.

So, not too many problems ahead, Sadie reflected dryly as she walked around the beautifully dressed dining tables she had arranged on the terrace outside to a meticulous plan. Satisfied with her final checks, she was able to stand for a moment looking out over the twinkling lights of the village far below. It was a perfect summer's evening for a celebration. The sky was a deep midnight blue, and the Milky Way was like a gauzy chiffon scarf billowing overhead. Fairy lights strung high above the tables competed with diamond stars crowning the snowy peaks of the Sierra Nevada, while crystal and silver, polished to the highest sheen, glinted on crisp white damask lit by mellow candlelight. All in all, the scene was beautifully warm and inviting.

The guests would arrive soon, Sadie reminded herself as she snapped into action, and she had yet to see Alejandro. Maria had said he would be checking the final details for the flamenco performance after dinner tonight. Sadie could picture him reassuring everyone and encouraging the performers to give of their best. She was looking forward to the show. The only snag was that it would take them into the early hours of the morning, cutting down her opportunities to speak to Alejandro.

At least he trusted her with arranging his party. Finally satisfied she'd done everything possible to please even the most discerning guest, Sadie returned to a kitchen that was now sparkling and efficient, with every conceivable appliance on hand to help Alejandro's staff. As she settled into the rhythm of cooking, every thought seemed to lead back to him. Would he like the menu—how she'd designed the kitchen—the way she had decorated the tables—the flowers, the candles, the special touches like the small personal gifts she'd put on each place setting? This was the biggest private occasion she'd handled to date, and she was keen to improve on anything she'd done before, so Alejandro's guests remembered the night as a momentous occasion, as it would be for them when she told him about the baby.

She was out on the terrace, quietly supervising the service of canapés and champagne to a group of early guests, when the performers began to arrive. Sadie knew some of them already and greeted them with hugs and smiles.

The women's brilliantly coloured dresses were hidden for now behind black capes. The men also wore capes over their severe black outfits as a type of uniform. The dancers' air of professional dignity spread excitement throughout the assembled guests. But Sadie was beginning to panic. Where was Alejandro? He was never late.

Discreet enquiries reassured her that he had stayed behind at the flamenco camp to make sure that everyone had transport both to and from the party. They'd had their differences but she had seen this caring side to Alejandro, and only hoped it would come to the fore when she told him her news. Each meeting between them was combative and exciting, but this time would be different, because so many hopes and dreams were wrapped up in his reaction.

Sadie's table plan placed Alejandro between his sisters, Annalisa and Marissa. No one could have fiercer bodyguards, she reflected wryly. Both women were lovely, and she hoped they'd share her joy. The sound of a helicopter approaching interrupted these thoughts and silenced the buzz of conversation on the terrace. As everyone stared up, Sadie shaded her eyes against the landing lights of the sleek black aircraft as it descended slowly to its roost on the top of the building.

The crackle of rotor blades and the rush of the wind they created threatened to put out the candles she'd lit, but somehow they survived. Having been flattened and almost extinguished by the arrival of the noble Duke, they sprang back to life and seemed to blaze more brightly than ever. As she must, Sadie determined as the impossibly good-looking father of her child jogged nonchalantly down the steps from the roof to join his guests.

In form-fitting trousers and a crisp white shirt open at the neck, and with a pale linen jacket slung over his shoulder, Alejandro was the epitome of style. She, red-faced from cooking, with her hair hidden behind a tight-fitting cap and sensible kitchen clogs on her feet, couldn't have provided a greater contrast. She could only imagine the type of child they'd produce. A tomboy, she suspected, if they had a girl, who would have laughing eyes and a stubborn chin, and possibly a shock of red curls, while a boy would no doubt stretch her nerves to breaking point with his daredevil antics.

Her heart turned over as Alejandro, who was surrounded by admirers, found her on the fringes of the crowd and flashed a look that scorched her from the inside out. Never had a more contrasting couple come together to produce a child, Sadie suspected with a brief acknowledging smile as she hurried back to her duties in the kitchen.

The event was a huge success. Annalisa insisted on leading the boisterous guests in noisy appreciation of Chef Sadie. The only person to remain silent throughout was Alejandro, but he was quiet in the way a volcano simmered before exploding into life. Each time she left the kitchen to check the progress of the banquet, he was watching her. She was tuned to him, and he to her. He was the flame, and she was—if not the moth, then in serious danger of getting her fingers burned.

Standing in the shadows to applaud the parade of Baked Alaska puddings as they left the kitchen, Sadie became hotly conscious of the fact that, as the guests watched the waiters carrying the dishes on high, Alejandro was watching Sadie.

Something had to give. *Someone.* Her body made a few honeyed suggestions. She ignored them. There was too much at stake for her to be distracted from her purpose tonight, which was to tell him about the baby, and when he left the table, she followed him into the house.

Feeling her behind him, he halted in the hall and turned to face her. 'Why have you been blocking my calls?'

'You—'

'I *what*?' he snapped, making her jump. His manner not what she'd hoped it would be when they began this conversation. 'I seem to remember you walked out on me. What was that about, Sadie? Keeping count? Hitting back? What type of childish game did you think you were playing?'

He was right, so she didn't pick him up on that point. 'I did try to call you, but you were away, I was told.'

'I'm often called away at a moment's notice,' Alejandro told her in a cold and distant voice that chilled her through. 'That's the nature of my business. I have responsibilities across the world.'

So, no time for a baby, Sadie thought, her hopes for some variation on the theme of happy family shattered. 'You didn't try to contact me,' she countered.

'As a matter of fact, I did,' he argued. 'I wanted to make sure you were okay, but you blocked my calls, so, we're quits,' he said coolly.

Did she really want to argue with him? 'I'm sorry.'

'And so am I,' he admitted, and sincerely, she thought.

They stared at each other long and hard until music sliced through the heavy silence. 'Shouldn't you be watching the performance with your guests?' she asked tensely.

Alejandro shrugged. 'I watched the dress rehearsal, so I know how good they are.'

'Maybe they'd appreciate your attendance,' she suggested.

His lips pressed down as he considered this. 'The performers' concentration is so profound,' he explained, 'that they wouldn't even know I was there.'

'Still—'

'Must you challenge every word I say?'

The tone was sharp, but a touch of humour had crept into his eyes that both thrilled and warmed her. So many feelings were swirling inside her head, making her wish they could start over with a clean, blank sheet.

'If you want to talk to me,' he said, 'I suggest we talk in here—'

It was the closest door, and it opened onto his fabulous leisure block. The space was vast and shady, with blue safety lights reflecting on the tranquil water of a massive swimming pool. It was the most amazing facility, with clusters of comfortably padded loungers arranged around the edge.

'Sadie...'

Before she had chance to take it all in, Alejandro drew her into his arms. Contact between them was always electric, but today it seemed stronger than ever. Perhaps because of the baby joining them, though Alejandro gave her no chance to dwell on this thought before kissing her until nothing was left except him.

'You need me,' he husked in her ear, his hunger raw and obvious. 'You need this...'

It wasn't a question, but a statement of fact, and as he cupped her she rubbed herself against him.

'Does that moan signal your agreement that, in the short time I can spare from the party, we should stop arguing, and, in fact, do a lot more than talk?' Alejandro suggested with a curving smile on his lips.

Plundering her mouth, he lifted her. Holding her close against him, he slowly lowered her so she knew how aroused he was. She was too... more than she could bear. Whatever passed between them, laughter, anger, disagreements, misunderstandings, Alejandro could always set her senses on fire.

He removed her thong at the same time as her comfortable chef's trousers. Freeing himself, he took her firmly in one deep thrust. She bathed in sensation as he supported her buttocks in his big, roughened hands and encouraged her to wrap her legs around his waist. Moans of need poured from her throat, as she worked with him until release came in a series of powerful spasms. Her screams of pleasure bounced over the tiled walls and by the time the echo had started to fade she was whimpering again as Alejandro kept on moving. He maintained a steady and dependable rhythm that made it easy for Sadie to claim her reward.

'Once more, I think,' he murmured when she was finally capable of hearing him, 'and then we must have that talk you asked for, before I return to my guests.'

Something in his eyes made her uneasy, but only for as long as it took Alejandro to carry her across to one of the sunbeds, where he sat down with his legs spread wide over the edges. Arranging her on top of him, he helped her to very slowly sink down. The angle of pleasure was the best it had ever been. Resting her head against the hard muscles of his chest, she moved her hips with his until he upped the speed and she couldn't hold on and fell gratefully and noisily into a starburst of sensation beyond which nothing else could exist.

'Better now?' he asked with amusement when she was quiet again. But he was still moving, still gently buffeting her all too eager body until she had no alternative but to feed it again.

'I don't think either of us is ever completely satisfied,' he growled softly with approval when at last she collapsed against him, panting with contentment. But when he went to pull away, she took over, and, tightening her inner muscles around him, she made Alejandro groan.

'You wanted to talk to me,' he reminded her when they were showering down in adjoining cubicles, 'and I haven't forgotten, but I've been away from my guests long enough, so it will have to wait until first thing tomorrow morning.'

Sadie tensed at the thought of another delay and all of her own making. 'I'd rather it was tonight.'

'It must be something important,' Alejandro commented.

They both turned off their showers in the same moment. 'It is,' she admitted, lifting her chin to face him as they stepped out of the stalls. Reaching for a towel, Alejandro slung it around her shoulders, before grabbing another to wrap around his waist. His silence unnerved her. Could he have guessed that she was expecting his child?

'I'm pregnant,' she said, before Alejandro had chance to seize the initiative.

'I should have guessed,' he said in a tone she couldn't read. 'What else could be so urgent?'

'I only just found out.'

'Even so…' he frowned deeply '…if I'd known, we wouldn't have made love so vigorously.'

As Alejandro's fierce love of family blazed from his eyes Sadie's insecurities rushed to the fore. Impending motherhood made it imperative that she fight off her doubts. A drive to protect and love was all part of expecting a baby. 'I have done my research,' she admitted, 'and regular sex poses no danger to the unborn child.'

'You checked?' Alejandro repeated incredulously. 'How long have you known?'

'Literally hours,' she said, 'and the instant I found out I researched everything on the Internet. I can't ask my mother, and none of my friends have had babies, but I'm not entirely helpless. I'm quite capable of reading up on things and asking questions. I do know something about caring for another human being, and nothing would induce me to take a chance with my baby's life.'

'You make this sound as if you plan to go it alone.'

'Why shouldn't I?' Sadie asked, frowning.

Alejandro's grim expression gradually softened. 'Why can't you trust me?' he asked, his hands gentle on her shoulders. 'I'll admit, I'm busy, and, not being used to accounting for my travels, I don't always quote chapter and verse where my itinerary is concerned, but that doesn't mean I don't care.'

'What do you expect from me, Alejandro?'

He shrugged and looked at her with compassion. 'That you break out of this cycle of self-loathing. You don't have to be alone. Reach out, seek help…from me.'

'But I'm fine on my own. I always have been,' she insisted.

Thinking how vulnerable she must look, barefoot and wrapped in a towel, and that this must have prompted Alejandro's concern, Sadie grabbed her clothes and held them in front of her.

'Asking for help doesn't make you weak,' Alejandro insisted. 'You're stronger than you think— No—don't turn away from me,' he said as she tried to slip past him. 'Match me— fight me—demand that I listen to you and understand how you feel. Don't hide away and refuse to take my calls. If you have big news, I'll drop everything. Feel free to air even the smallest concern. All I ask is that you're open with me, and trust me, and that you listen to someone else's point of view before you decide anything. We've had a misunderstanding, but how can that be considered relevant by either of us, in light of this incredible news?'

As he spoke, Alejandro brought her back to face him. 'I want you to accept how much *you* have to offer *me*, and then put the past behind you once and for all.'

'So, you're not angry about the baby?'

'Angry?' Closing his eyes as if he needed to take a moment, Alejandro appeared bemused when he opened them again. 'Far from it. I couldn't be more thrilled. My only concern is that you will have to make some serious adjustments.'

'As will you,' Sadie countered.

'Welcome changes,' Alejandro stated firmly. 'I intend to take a full part in my child's life.'

'Our child,' she said, feeling a flutter of alarm as they maintained eye contact.

As Alejandro gave a brisk nod of agreement, she accepted that pregnancy had heightened her emotions, and that perhaps she should take a step back. Passions rose quickly between them, even more so now, making it easy to jump to the wrong conclusion.

'Are you reassured?' Alejandro probed with a frown.

'Yes,' she admitted cautiously. 'I'm just getting used to the fact that you're as thrilled with the news as I am.'

'I'm not sure you'll be able to dance in those clogs,' he observed wryly as she dipped down to slip them back on.

'I wish I could spare the time to dance, but I've got too much left to do.'

'And a kitchen full of helpers,' he reminded her, 'all of whom you have trained in excellence to the nth degree. I don't know anyone more organised than you, which on this occasion plays to my advantage,' he added dryly, 'so we dance, to celebrate the news of a new life. That's what my people do. That's what flamenco is. The music speaks for us, expressing our emotions.'

Expressing emotions *for* him, she thought, which was probably another reason why Alejandro found it so hard, if not impossible to verbalise his feelings. Cut him some slack, she thought as she closed her eyes to take stock for a moment. They'd just shared some of the most life-changing news possible, and he'd taken it far better than she could ever have imagined. Was she really going to challenge him now?

CHAPTER THIRTEEN

'WHY DON'T YOU return to your room first?' Alejandro suggested. 'Dancing in chef's whites with clogs on your feet might prove a bit restricting.'

'To put it mildly,' Sadie agreed, feeling a smile growing as the tension between them evaporated.

'Don't rush,' Alejandro encouraged. 'I'll be with my guests, and I'll wait for you.'

'Thanks.' Ideally, she would have liked to talk first and dance later, but Alejandro had been away from his guests long enough.

Opening the door to her suite, Sadie gasped with surprise. Only one person could have arranged this, but how had Alejandro found the time? The answer sat on a gilded console table, where a note on stiff card was attached to the most fabulous floral display of white roses and fragrant orange blossom she'd ever seen.

Welcome back. As soon as I learned your plans I had florists and designers on standby, waiting for my call. I hope you're pleased with the result.

Beneath his signature, he'd added,

I can't thank you enough for making everything easier for my staff. Maria, for one, says you've revolutionised her working life.

Pleased? That didn't come close to how she felt, knowing she'd been in Alejandro's thoughts all along. Hugging the note close, emotion sweeping over her, she thought what Castillo Fuego had come to mean, along with everyone who worked there, and, yes, the owner too. She loved everything about Alejandro's magnificent mountain home, and at times like these even felt that she belonged here, but this wasn't her home. The magnificent dwelling wasn't anyone's home. It was

just another of Alejandro's impressive pos-
sessions. Was she to become one more? Was
their child—?

Stop that now! If she carried those thoughts
any further the past really would mess up her
life. She was her own person, and always
would be. The fact that she was falling in love
with Alejandro de Alegon was up to Sadie
to control, but he made it hard with touching
gifts like this, when she hadn't wanted or expected anything, and was only doing her job.

But the next thing she spotted was a rail of
gowns fit for a princess. With an excited ex-
clamation of surprise, she hurried across the
room to run her fingertips along the range of
rainbow-hued dresses. Silks, chiffon, crepe,
satin and lace hung in tempting profusion.
How had he managed to organise all of this in
one day? Proof positive that no one ever said
no to a request from Alejandro! People had
clearly gone to a lot of trouble on her behalf
so, surely, it wouldn't hurt to try them on...?

So, she was going to dance with Alejandro?

Of course! Or have him think she was chick-
ening out. And she would be wearing one of

these fabulous gowns. He'd been extremely thoughtful, and it would be churlish not to.

Is he wooing you with all the special things you could have if you agree to come under his wing?

No. He's being thoughtful.

Sadie argued firmly with her inner doubt demon. She wouldn't be able to wear any of these in a few months' time, and it would take far more courage to give birth and raise a child than it would to put on one of these pretty dresses and return to the party.

Sadie was a gutsy woman, and he would have put money on her wearing one of the fabulous gowns he'd ordered from Paris when she came back to the party. What he couldn't have anticipated was quite how amazing she looked. Familiar with every contour of her body, he wondered how many of his guests had recognised the woman at the top of the steps as the earnest chef who'd prepared such a superb feast for them this evening. The *über*-professional was nowhere to be seen, and in her place was a flame-haired beauty.

She was wearing the minimum of make-up. The light in her face was all the enhancement needed. Vibrant auburn locks cascaded to her waist, and she had chosen to wear the gown he'd hoped she would. Nude-coloured lace with a pale peach silk lining, it was the most provocative on the rail, and clung to her form with such loving attention to detail she might as well have been naked. Like everyone else present he was transfixed by her charm, her poise and Sadie's remarkable colouring. No duchess could outshine her and, driven by the need to let every other man present know that he was staking his claim, he strode up the steps to greet her, and offered to escort her down. 'You look fabulous,' he murmured as he linked their arms.

'I can walk down a few steps on my own,' she told him wryly.

'In those heels?'

Slipping them off, she linked her arm through his again.

'You annoying, extraordinary woman,' he ground out beneath his breath.

'Annoying?' she queried. 'Were the gowns

left to tease me? Was I supposed to stay in my room?'

'Like Cinderella?' he suggested. 'Now there's a role that definitely doesn't suit you.'

She shrugged. 'But thank you for making me feel so good tonight. I love the dresses... every one of them, and, whether you like it or not,' she added with a breathtaking smile, 'you have made me feel like Cinderella.'

Was that good or bad? he wondered as he brought Sadie into his arms. He could never be quite sure with Sadie. Keeping him on his toes was a big part of her allure.

One sizzling dance later, during which he attempted to keep a dignified distance while Sadie's delectable body brushed mercilessly against his, they parted by mutual agreement to circulate amongst his guests.

'What a charming woman— How lovely she is— What a beauty—' came from all quarters as he moved around. It took his sister to inject some harsh reality into his thinking.

'Will you hang onto her this time?' Annalisa demanded. 'Or will you screw it up again?'

'I'll send you to bed without your supper, if you're not careful.'

'I'd like to see you try. But still,' Annalisa observed, cocking her head to weigh him up with narrowed eyes, 'hearing you make a joke is certainly an improvement. Sadie obviously has a good effect on you.'

Removing his sister's restraining hand from his arm, he managed to waylay a boisterous group of young men heading in Sadie's direction with the promise of a jeroboam of vintage champagne. He had never felt such a proprietary interest in a woman before, he realised as Annalisa shook her head in despair and walked away.

Sadie was expecting his child.

Yes, but this was something more than that. Was it possible he was falling in love with her?

Sadie really enjoyed talking to Alejandro's guests. They were an interesting group of people. Of course, there were snobs at the party, but they were in the minority, and even the stuffiest managed to unbend when she treated them like all the rest. When the dancing started up again, she and Alejandro seemed drawn to each other like pieces in a puzzle that fitted each other exactly.

'Happy?' he asked as they moved instinctively in time to the sultry rhythms of Spain.

'Very.' But when this was over, she wanted to hear him say that he would agree to be part of their baby's future without taking over every aspect of their child's upbringing.

She must learn the art of compromise too, Sadie conceded as the band segued into a slow tune and Alejandro drew her closer still. Since childhood, everything had seemed black and white. Black for loss of control, and white when she took it back again. Somehow, she had to learn to accept that there were infinite shades of grey.

He was a natural-born protector in danger of losing his job, Alejandro reflected dryly as Sadie insisted on leaving the dance floor to check on her colleagues in the kitchen. It was time to take action, but before he could sweep her up and carry her away to the mountain encampment they both loved, he had some business to attend to, which would eat up around a month of his time. He hadn't told Sadie yet, because it was a very recent addition to his diary, and, because their reunion was so tender and new, he wanted to break it to her gently. Learning he was to become a father had made him want to do everything he could to reassure Sadie and to make her feel secure. As soon as they were reunited in the more relaxed setting of the flamenco camp, he was confident he could persuade her to accept that life under his protection would be easier, and not at all confining—either for Sadie or their child.

He was accustomed to taking charge of everything, and as he mingled amongst his guests he found himself glancing constantly in the direction of the kitchen. How long was she going to be away from the party? Passionate, vulnerable and yet so strong, Sadie was a captivating mix of contradictions that he found utterly compelling. The changes in a woman during pregnancy couldn't be denied, and Sadie appeared more entrenched than ever in the belief that only she could steer a safe passage through life. If only he could convince her that there was another way.

Remembering how his mother had rejoiced when she was carrying Annalisa, he wanted the same happiness for Sadie. But his mother had enjoyed all the things Sadie lacked, like the support of her family in the mountains, and his father fussing over her every minute of the day. She had been free to enjoy the excitement of impending motherhood, as Sadie should, but Sadie didn't want or need him to steer her course. The part of him that was pure, primitive male demanded she must— or at least make him the first call if she needed help—but nothing was ever that simple with Sadie.

Sadie smiled with relief, knowing her first professional party was a huge success. As she had predicted, it went on long into the night. By the time the last guest had departed, and she had made sure each member of staff was safely on their way home, she finally admitted she was exhausted and more than ready for bed.

Alejandro waylaid her at the front door and, kissing her on both cheeks, thanked her for a wonderful night. Professional, or personal, she wondered as he cupped her face as if she were a precious china doll who might break if he kissed her too hard.

'I'm pregnant, not sick,' she teased as she smiled up into his blisteringly handsome face.

'Allow me to be tender sometimes,' he said. 'I'm still getting used to our news. And now you need some rest,' he insisted, stepping back. 'You've worked so hard tonight. If I'd known what you were planning, I would have stopped you.'

'Oh, for goodness' sake, Alejandro, I won't break. Women work right up to the birth, as I shall.'

Alejandro frowned and said nothing. 'You'll have to see how you're feeling at the time,' he finally conceded.

'Of course I will,' she said as he kissed her again.

This kiss was so long and lingering, she shivered involuntarily because it felt like goodbye.

'Are you going somewhere again?' she asked when he released her.

'Would you miss me?'

'Of course.'

'And you wouldn't do anything silly while I'm away?'

'You are going,' she said with certainty. 'So, how long is it this time?' She had no right to ask, but the words had shot out of her mouth before she could stop them, and now she regretted each and every syllable, because they made her sound desperate, when she relied on no one and never had.

'I can't tell you how long I'm going to be exactly,' Alejandro admitted, 'but I'm always on the other end of the phone, so don't turn yours off this time.'

Nothing had changed, Sadie reflected, feeling as if a big black hole had just opened up in her stomach. Alejandro continued to live as if he was accountable to no one, and the truth of it was he was right. She had no call on him, though she felt sick to the stomach at the thought of him leaving. In fairness, she had needed space to get used to the idea of a baby, but what if Alejandro needed space from her? Glibly promising that she would forget the past was one thing, but someone should tell that wretched worm of doubt inside her to stop twisting and turning.

'Go get some sleep. You must be exhausted. I'll be leaving in a few hours' time, so I won't disturb you.'

So not even the prospect of one last night, wrapped in each other's arms.

'Sadie…' Dipping his head, Alejandro stared into her eyes. 'I *am* coming back, and until I do I want you to rest here. With Maria to look after you, you couldn't be in a better place.'

'I can't stay here. What about my job in Madrid?'

'Resign.'

'That isn't an option for me.'

'And when the baby's born?'

'I'll sort something out.'

They stared at each other in silence before finally accepting that neither of them was about to give way, and then Sadie dragged her gaze away from Alejandro's and returned alone to her room.

After a restless few hours' dozing, she heard the helicopter taking off. Rushing to the window, she stared out as the powerful machine soared overhead and wheeled away. Alejandro was giving her space she *had* thought she needed, but she didn't want it now; she wanted him. They still had to talk about the baby and plan the future...unless Alejandro didn't think it necessary to consider the future, because he would decide, he would plan, he would instruct— No! The baby joined them, but everything was going to be different from Sadie's experience as a child. She'd make sure of it.

To anchor herself, she called Chef Sorollo to tell him the news, and as soon as he heard about the baby he insisted she must take a sabbatical to coincide with her pregnancy. She agreed that it was time to step out of her insular existence in Madrid, to discover more about the other side of her baby's heritage, and she didn't have to wait for Alejandro to help her do that. She'd always been strong, and now it was time to use that strength.

As Marissa and Annalisa were spending time together in Madrid, Sadie's obvious destination was the flamenco camp. She wasn't interested in resting, as Alejandro had suggested. She felt fit and well, and there was no reason why she couldn't carry on researching recipes and traditions in the mountains. Her body would tell her when she'd done enough, and she would rest when that time came. She wasn't worried about arriving unannounced at the camp, or being without her friends Annalisa and Marissa, because cooking, like music, brought people together across the world, and this was the best chance she'd get to learn more about the customs of the people that through Alejandro's mother had enriched the de Alegon line.

Telling Maria where she was going, she packed her bags. Taking one last look around her fabulous suite of rooms, she left the building to hitch a lift up to the flamenco camp with a group of gardeners who were heading there within the hour. Returning to the community she loved was something she looked forward to, though whether it would take her mind off Alejandro... Staring up at the sky, she wished she didn't miss him quite so much already.

The call shocked him out of bed at two in the morning. Like all middle-of-the-night calls, it had far more impact than if he'd received the same news at two in the afternoon, when the world was a livelier, brighter place, and his brain was firing on all cylinders. Receiver jammed between ear and shoulder, he logged the vital information as he tugged on his jeans. A disaster had struck the flamenco camp.

And Sadie was there! Pregnant Sadie. Sadie, pregnant with his baby!

What the hell was she doing at the flamenco camp? Why wasn't she resting at his house in the mountains as he had instructed? He'd planned on her relaxing until he returned, and in a safe and secure place where she would be well looked after by Maria. He'd only had a couple of hours' sleep, and his business was nowhere near concluded, but he'd meant it when he'd told Sadie that she wasn't alone. Buckling his belt, he called to file an emergency flight plan. With any luck he'd arrive at the flamenco camp before dawn.

An avalanche in the height of summer wasn't unusual in this part of Spain, Sadie learned as she checked on the well-being of a huddle of people who were sheltering beneath an overhang in the cliff. The rapid rise in temperature had melted the snow at the summit, and high winds had added to the problem, making the surface snow unstable.

The first Sadie had known of impending disaster was when the whisper of trouble she had thought was merely a change in the direction of the wind became a roar that tipped the guest caravan where she was sleeping onto its side, spilling Sadie out of bed onto a cold, hard floor. Once she was over the shock, she checked herself over and gave herself a moment to be sure that her tumble hadn't harmed the baby. Then, finding her clothes amidst the jumble of assorted belongings that had hit the floor, which wasn't hard, as most of them had fallen on top of her, she dressed quickly and forced a window open so she could climb out and see who needed help.

Slithering down the side of the upturned caravan, Sadie scrambled to her feet and looked around. A scene of complete devastation greeted her. The usually sun-drenched plateau had been transformed into a winter wonderland, but there was nothing funny or entertaining about this snow-covered scene, because people's homes had been wrecked, and both children and adults were moving slowly around the site in a daze. If there was one thing she was good at, it was organisation. Without it, the most talented chefs would soon crash and burn. Having alerted the authorities and left a text on Alejandro's phone when he didn't pick up, she set to work. Discovering the extent of the damage to people and property was the first priority. Setting up a triage station manned by those with nursing skills was the next. Reuniting families was crucial, and, for the sake of children, the elderly and the injured, it needed to happen fast.

Delegating where possible, she liaised with the surprising number of people who had stepped up to help, issuing each of them with precise instructions as to where their help could best be utilised. Previously, her welcome at the camp had been friendly and polite, but now she was made to feel that she belonged.

CHAPTER FOURTEEN

HE ARRIVED WITH not one, but three helicopters, ready to evacuate the camp. As the
aircraft he was piloting swooped lower, he
spotted a young woman, red hair flying as
she gestured to those who'd marked out a safe
landing site in the snow to stand clear.

'Sadie?'

He was astounded to find her apparently di-
recting the start of a clear-up operation. *What
the hell?* She was pregnant and should be resting. Calling up his PA, he asked him to alert
the best obstetrician in Madrid to expect a
new patient. Mountain rescue had already confirmed they were on their way with a fleet of
service aircraft, and his fleet of private helicopters was in the air. Hovering over the
landing cross, which the indomitable Sadie
no doubt had marked out clearly on top of

the snow, he brought the aircraft down and switched off the engine.

Appearing totally in control of the situation, she strode to meet him. The scolding he'd intended to give her was lost in the briefing she gave him as briskly as she might any other emergency professional in the field. 'Initial stages of the rescue are well under way,' she said when she'd finished the update, meeting his stern stare levelly.

Having reassured himself that she did look in the best of health, and had possibly never looked better, he replied in the same brisk tone, 'Good job. Command centre?'

'Your caravan, I'm afraid. It was one of the few structures left undamaged, thanks to its sheltered position in the encampment.'

'No problem. How are you?' he said, asking the question at the forefront of his mind. He stared at her intently as they strode along.

She glanced at him briefly. 'I'm fine. The baby's fine. I can assure you that I haven't overdone it or taken any risks.'

'You just initiated a full-scale rescue operation,' he argued. 'Was that safe, in your opinion?'

'Would you rather I had sat it out?'

'In your condition? Yes.'

Her glance this time was full of steel. 'I'm okay, Alejandro.'

'I guess you are,' he conceded grimly.

'This is what I've arranged so far,' she said, turning the spotlight away from herself.

It was hard to believe quite how comprehensive Sadie's report was. He had never admired her more, though she was one infuriatingly self-willed woman.

'I hope you don't mind,' she said as they arrived at his caravan. 'It's also bigger than the rest of the homes, so requisitioning this particular van was the obvious choice.'

'I don't mind at all. It couldn't have been put to a better use. Just tell me you haven't done any of the heavy lifting,' he ground out as he glanced at the piles of supplies that had already been air-dropped into camp.

'You can trust me to do what's right,' she said firmly.

But could she trust him, and what would it take to make that happen?

'Come and meet the team,' she said, opening the door to his caravan.

It was almost as if they were partners, he thought as the rest of the team greeted them and offered seats to him and Sadie so they sat side by side at the head of the table. This was most definitely a partnership like no other he'd ever known, and he welcomed Sadie's robust manner because it got things done. She wasn't afraid to challenge him, and, apart from all the good ideas that she'd put into operation, she'd proved herself to be more than level-headed in a crisis.

She was a mass of contradictions, he concluded. When it came to anything personal, Sadie's illogical side could so easily kick in. Maybe that would always be part of her persona. And maybe that was what made her so interesting, and such a challenge. Would he change her? Probably not, he conceded as the meeting ended and they stepped outside. All he could do was love her and make her feel safe. There was nothing in the world he wanted more than a stand-up woman who could, and who would, take him on, as Sadie did.

They had slept on their feet, or that was what it felt like, Sadie thought as she boiled up some water for coffee on the campfire she'd built outside the caravan. The army rescue team had set up a feeding station, and they all greeted Alejandro with enthusiasm, having remembered him from his time in Special Forces, which was another thing she'd just learned about him. The level of testosterone swirling around that tent had been too much to deal with, so she'd slipped away to make a campfire of her own.

'Enough for two?'

Whirling around, she discovered Alejandro standing behind her. That was enough to send her senses rioting. In full, tough work gear, with his thick black hair tangled and powdered with snow, and his stubble so sharp and black he looked like a pirate, it was unfair to look so good in this type of situation.

'You look great, considering the work you've

put in since you arrived,' she said with her customary frankness. 'And there's plenty for two.'

'Then, coffee would be good,' he said as he hunkered down beside her.

He was way too much of a distraction when there was still so much work to do. 'I can only take a short break,' she explained.

'Long enough, I hope?' As he said this Alejandro's stare levelled on her face. When she chose not to answer, he pulled her close. 'You've done a great job, but now it's time for you to step back, and let others take over.'

'Are you patronising me?'

'No. I'm being properly careful with your health,' he argued. 'What you've done here won't be forgotten by anyone.'

'I'll go down in myth and legend?' she suggested wryly, stifling a yawn. 'Seriously, I'm just one of many. Everyone helped out.'

'But you helped them over the initial shock by giving direction. They needed something to do to feel they were working towards the recovery of the camp, and you did that.'

'They still need me around,' Sadie insisted, feeling she'd taken too much time out already.

'*I* need you around.'

Her glance flew to his mouth. He had a very sexy mouth, and, though she was loath to admit it, pregnancy had made her mad for sex; whatever their differences, Alejandro had taught her the difference between sex with him and no sex with him.

'Sit,' he insisted when she cancelled her disturbing thoughts in favour of action of a far more practical type. 'Really—I mean it—sit down. The next shift's taken over, and they've got everything under control.'

She hesitated for a few moments, and then sat down again.

They were sitting on hessian sacks in the snow in front of the campfire she'd built. It was warm in front of the fire, and things were starting to return to normal in the camp. In addition to the staff and equipment Alejandro and the army had provided, dozens of volunteers from neighbouring villages had rallied round with tents and blankets, food and a seemingly endless supply of strong, hot coffee.

'I've opened up Castillo Fuego,' Alejandro

told her, 'so until they get their lives in order again, all the people here will have a home.'

'That's a fantastic thing to do.'

'You're fantastic,' he said.

Helicopters buzzed overhead like a never-ending swarm of noisy insects as they ferried in fresh supplies. A more romantic setting would be hard to find, Sadie reflected dryly as Alejandro smoothed her hair.

'Seriously, you must take a break,' he said. 'You held the fort until everyone got here, and you've done a fantastic job. Please, take some of the praise,' he insisted when Sadie shook her head. 'Or must I persuade you?'

'Oh, persuade me, I think,' she said.

Alejandro had never needed much encouragement, and neither had she. Moving into his arms, she thrust her fingers through his hair to bind him close. When he brushed her lips with his, then teased them apart to deepen the kiss, she was lost, and so was he. Hunger consumed them. How they didn't make love on the snow, with any passer-by who cared to do so watching them, would remain one of life's mysteries for ever. Relief that they were both safe and unharmed, and full of determination to carry on and help out, help each other, only added fuel to a fierce, raging fire.

'You take far too much for granted,' she teased when finally they came up for air.

'You think?' Alejandro demanded softly.

'You are a very bad man,' she said.

'I couldn't agree more,' Alejandro told her as he dragged her close for another kiss.

With the resilience typical of Alejandro's people, the flamenco camp was soon up and running again with music playing and people dancing, while others took it in turns to shovel snow. Sadie and Alejandro were amongst the shovellers. Whether he approved or not, she knew what she could do and what she mustn't attempt, and she was determined to listen to her body where that was concerned.

'Dance?' he suggested, his energy seemingly not even dented by the exercise.

Resting on her shovel, Sadie glanced around. 'How can we?'

'Put one foot in front of the other—preferably in time to the music,' he suggested dryly.

'We've nearly cleared the snow, and there've been no serious injuries. Everyone knows how lucky the encampment has been. They want to celebrate, and we should too. You've done enough work for today,' he added, taking the shovel from her hands.

Planting her hands on her hips, Sadie angled her chin to challenge him with a look, but Alejandro's macho expression made her laugh. 'What do I have to do,' she asked him, 'to train you in the gentle art of letting go of the reins from time to time?'

'Says you,' he exclaimed with incredulity.

'I guess we're as bad as each other,' she admitted, standing down.

'So we dance,' he said.

There would be no miraculous changes in Don Alejandro de Alegon just yet, Sadie reflected with amusement as Alejandro drew her into his arms, but they did have a lot to celebrate. And, having attended some beginner's flamenco classes while she was living in the encampment, she had a few new moves to try out.

'Nothing too vigorous,' Alejandro warned as she headed for the stage.

'I'm sure I can rely on you to curb my wilder instincts,' she teased. 'Or maybe not,' she added, flashing a glance at Alejandro.

Every part of her was pressed up against him, and, when he swung her around, his hands were firm on her body. 'I'm not letting you go,' he said as a couple next to them performed an intricate move that saw the woman bent over the man's arm until her long hair dusted the ground. 'Who knows what you might get up to?'

'I think you can trust me to interpret the music without risk to life and limb.'

'But this is more fun,' he said, bringing her closer still.

He did have a point, Sadie conceded, giving a mock growl of complaint, when actually there was nowhere else she'd rather be. But her satisfaction didn't last too long. 'Alejandro! Put me down again this instant!' she insisted when he carried her away to a chorus of cheers when the musicians dramatically upped the tempo of the music.

'I prefer something slower and more considered,' he said as he drew to a halt in front of his caravan.

'And now I'm going to claim back my caravan,' he said as he gently lowered her to the ground.

'You can't just move back in,' Sadie insisted as Alejandro strode purposefully towards the command centre she'd set up. 'I've requisitioned it.'

'And I'm countermanding your order,' he said. 'The army has established a perfectly adequate command centre, so no one's going to come back here. More crucially,' he added with a slanting glance, 'my caravan has a clean, undamaged bed, and you need to rest.'

'Rest?' Sadie protested. 'How can I rest when there's still so much work to be done?'

'I'll make you sleep,' Alejandro promised as he mounted the steps, entered the shady caravan, and closed the door behind them.

'I thought you said I had to rest?' Sadie protested excitedly, recognising the look in his eyes.

'You will rest when I've finished with you.'

With a promise like that, she had no intention of arguing, especially when Alejandro reminded her how good making love in bed could be.

'You have absolutely no scruples,' she accused.

'None at all,' he agreed, and, flicking a lever on the wall, he brought a bed down. 'While we worked through the night, many of the volunteers grabbed some sleep, so now it's our turn to rest and recuperate.'

'Is that what you call it now?'

His laughing eyes made her smile as he explained, 'You will rest, while I recuperate— with enthusiasm, and exquisite attention to detail. I think that's a fair description.'

She laughed. 'I'm not going to argue with you.'

Sadie's body thrilled to feel Alejandro's pressing into her as he lowered her down on the bed. Unshaven in work-stained clothes, he was even more irresistible, and he was right about making love in bed. She had forgotten nothing.

Stroking her hand down his powerful back

as he swung out of bed a long time later to take a call, she realised how much she loved him, and had missed him.

'Trouble?' she asked, seeing him frown as he ended the call.

She should have known, Sadie realised, feeling that big black hole opening up again as he placed another call to book a flight plan back to Madrid.

'More supplies for the camp?' she asked worriedly.

'No. Everything's settled here. The army will be rehousing people whose homes have been destroyed, so there's no need for me to open Castillo Fuego. In fact, everything should return to normal within the next few hours. But it's something else,' he said.

'Not enough!' she insisted when he started to pull on his clothes. 'You can't leave me again without an explanation. We both have duties and responsibilities, and, though you're not used to talking about yours, if I mean anything to you, you must learn to share, as I must learn to trust. We both have hang-ups, but can't you see how they're linked? If you don't share with me, how can I trust you? And if I can't trust you, what kind of life is that going to be for our child? We *still* haven't talked about the baby, and we must.'

Alejandro's face was grimmer than she'd ever seen it. 'Annalisa has summoned me to Madrid,' he explained. 'She's broken off her engagement to the Prince.'

'Well, she must have a very good reason,' Sadie reasoned out loud. 'But why would she want to stay in Madrid? Maria told me that Marissa's on her way home to the flamenco camp, so Annalisa will have no one to stand beside her when the press gets wind of this. Send for her, Alejandro,' she begged. 'Bring her home to us where she's safe from the chatter in the city. Don't you always say, it's easier to see things clearly in the mountains?'

'You'd do that for my sister?' Alejandro said quietly.

'Of course I would,' Sadie confirmed. 'I'd do anything to help your family, and maybe it would help Annalisa to talk to another woman. I can't imagine she'd find it easy to confide in her brother. She's all grown up, Alejandro.

Annalisa isn't that same little girl. What you did for her was amazing, but you have to learn to let her go and stand back now.'

'I have to protect her,' he said, raking his hair. 'I always have, and I always will, and if that man's hurt her—'

'Of course, step in,' Sadie agreed, 'but I'm confident Annalisa can sort this out. Believe in your sister. With you for a brother, I don't think she can go far wrong. Allow her to take charge of her life, as we all must. I'm not going to hang around to see what fate decides for our baby, and neither should you.'

There were a few long moments of silence, and then Alejandro said abruptly, 'I'll cancel my flight.'

'You're not admitting I'm right, are you?' Sadie queried with a small, slanting smile.

Grabbing her close, Alejandro stared fiercely into her eyes. 'On this one occasion—all others are up for grabs.'

'Then, I'd better make sure I grab a few,' Sadie countered as she linked her hands behind Alejandro's neck to make sure he wasn't going anywhere.

* * *

As he watched the two women reunite on the steps of Castillo Fuego, he knew Sadie was right. There was something up here in the Sierra Nevada that made everything possible. Some called it magic. He called it peace and fresh air. Whatever it was, seeing his sister with Sadie to advise her made him happy, and clearly it made Annalisa happy too. Convincing Sadie to trust him, however, might turn out to be a longer and more complicated task.

Once his sister was settled in her room and Sadie had reappeared on the landing, he called up the stairs and suggested they saddle up and go for a ride so they could talk about the baby uninterrupted.

'Good idea,' Sadie agreed, but she was frowning when she joined him in the hall.

'You don't seem so keen?'

'I am. Absolutely,' she insisted. 'It's just that listening to Annalisa takes me back to my childhood and reminds me how unkind people can be to each other. Your sister doesn't deserve that. No one does.'

'Is there anything I can do to help?'

'Stay out of it,' Sadie advised. 'Unless Annalisa asks you for help. She's got this.'

He ground his jaw, knowing Sadie was discreet and loyal, and unlikely to part with any details. He'd have to wait for Annalisa to do that. 'How can you be so level-headed about everyone else, and yet still allow the past to haunt you?'

'Maybe I'm starting to lay those ghosts,' she said. 'And it's your turn next,' she challenged, smiling as they left the house and headed for the stables.

How could she know him so well, when his default setting had always prohibited the smallest show of feelings? How much he'd changed, Alejandro marvelled. Years of battling to keep things running smoothly for Annalisa and the business had accustomed him to keeping any personal concerns to himself, but with the arrival of Sadie in his life his thoughts and feelings were an open book. 'I know I'm tired of being alone.'

The words had shot from his mouth like bullets from a gun, and he doubted he could have shocked Sadie more. She hid it well as she suggested, 'Let's take that ride. I think we both need a chance to talk.'

CHAPTER FIFTEEN

THEY AMBLED ALONG, reins hanging loose, completely relaxed and chatting easily.

Of course she missed the flat-out gallops, but being pregnant meant being careful, and knowing the baby was safe was everything.

'Happy?' Alejandro asked.

'Of course.' He only had to turn to look at her for her heart to soar. Thinking about the day when she would introduce their child to this world of dramatic mountain scenery was all the happiness she needed. The shades and contrasts alone were incredible. Lavender mountains, green plains, stark grey granite cliffs, laced with silver and aquamarine ice, dazzled the eye, while tiny luminous white villages dotted the valley far below. There was something about the scale of their surroundings that put everything else in perspective. It freed the spirit to range far and wide and allowed the imagination to venture boldly. Talking about the past was suddenly easy. They even laughed together at her stubborn belief as a child that things should be better, and that it was up to Sadie to change things.

'You haven't changed a bit,' Alejandro teased.

She shrugged and smiled. 'I've just become more determined and driven.'

'But time out like this is good, isn't it?'

'Says you!'

They smiled at each other, and as Alejandro stared out across the trail, she thought it was by far the best thing of all to ride alongside the man she loved, the man who was a gypsy king and Spanish don, but to Sadie would always be Alejandro.

Just to make her senses a little more on edge, he'd tied a black bandana around his head to keep his thick wild hair out of his eyes. With that thick coating of sharp black stubble on his jaw and wearing old jeans, he had never looked more attractive. A tight-fitting top emphasised his muscular physique, so, all in all, he gave the mountain scenery a run for its money. With no appointments to keep, or meals to prepare, they allowed the horses to set the pace. It was just the two of them, and their thoughts and hopes for the future.

All I want is to be with you, Sadie thought, and that would be with Alejandro the man, not the hard-driven billionaire. *I want this amazingly sexy, funny, honest, deep-thinking man to be a father to my child, the man who worries so much about other people that he never has time to consider the possibility of someone caring about him, worrying about him.*

'Your thoughts for the future?' he prompted.

'With you,' she said bluntly, 'but I always was a dreamer.'

'Not just a dreamer,' he argued. 'You get things done.' He slanted her a look. 'Should I be worried?'

'I hope so.'

He laughed and their combined laughter rang out in the clean mountain air.

'I suppose there's no point in my warning you that I have a very different life in Madrid?'

'Like me, do you mean?' she said. 'I get that.'

'So, where does that leave us?' he asked, reining in.

'Independent but together.'

He smiled. 'I like the sound of that.

'You like sex too.'

'I love sex.'

'And you love the thought of being a father,' she said, bringing her horse alongside his, 'but this has to be something more than that.'

'How can you say that? How can you even think it?'

Dismounting, he brought her into his arms. 'Don't doubt me,' he whispered against her lips.

Making love in the open air could become a habit Sadie wouldn't want to kick. They tethered their horses, and by the time Alejandro had gently lowered her to the ground, she was ready. But this time she wanted more.

'What?' Alejandro murmured, his dark eyes searching hers. 'Tell me what you want. I'll give you anything.'

'I want everything,' she said. 'I want all of you—not just the amazing sex and the banter between us, and certainly not your fabulous lifestyle.'

'Slaving away in my kitchen, do you mean?' he teased.

Sadie was in no mood to be distracted. The time had come to tell Alejandro exactly how she felt and take the consequences whatever they might be. 'It's all or nothing,' she said.

Alejandro's lips pressed down in a way that had always melted her heart. 'That's a big ask,' he said, eyes searching and smiling and speculating, all at the same time.

She smiled and shrugged, to try and make it seem that her whole life didn't depend on his answer. 'If your answer is nothing, we can still make plans for the baby. I'll draw up a schedule of visits, and I promise to consult you on every decision I make regarding our child's future—'

'Stop,' he said. 'Every decision *you* make?'

'I'll consult you first,' Sadie protested, thinking that quite fair.

'On the decisions *you* make,' Alejandro repeated, frowning. 'I think you'll find it doesn't work like that.'

'Then, what will work for you?' she asked.

Could they really be this far apart? Alejandro wondered.

Yes, because you can't bring yourself to open up, any more than Sadie can allow trust into her life. Say it—tell her how you feel about her right now or regret the missed opportunity for ever.

'I love you, Sadie Montgomery.' Stroking her hair back from her face, he admitted, 'I'm only sorry it's taken me this long to tell you how much I love you. I guess I'm no better at expressing my feelings than you've been at holding them in today.'

'I'm one up on you, at least,' she whispered. 'I love you more than you know. I can't believe I found you.'

'Nor I you.'

'Poor you,' she said. 'I bet you wish you'd dodged out of the way.'

'Seriously, Sadie, I'm lucky to have you in my life.'

'But don't feel obligated,' she whispered. 'I can do this without you. No pressure.'

'No pressure, and none required,' he confirmed. 'I've no doubt you can achieve anything you set your mind to. But do you want to do everything on your own? I know I don't. I used to, until you showed me a different way.'

'A crotchety, combative, challenging way, do you mean?' she suggested with a cheeky grin.

'A healthy, vibrant, open way,' he argued.

'You love me,' Sadie confirmed, frowning deeply as she searched his eyes.

'Yes. Why is that so hard to believe? From now on you can step back sometimes, and I'll be there to support you. You don't have to be strong all the time. Parenting between couples is a partnership…or it should be.'

'You've changed,' she murmured.

'And so have you,' he pointed out. 'We're both in the process of changing. Baby steps,' he teased with a smile.

The silence was longer this time. Not for one second did Sadie's gaze flicker as she studied his eyes. And then she smiled and relaxed. 'Baby steps with your feet?'

He shrugged. 'So long as they don't land in my mouth.'

'But, what if I can't?' she said, frowning again.

'Can't what?'

'Be a good mother?' she explained worriedly. 'You have the example of a happy family to look back on and copy.'

'While you have all the tools necessary to make sure you avoid the mistakes of the past. Come on, Sadie, you're better than this. You never let anything get on top of you in the past.'

'Except you.'

He grinned and shifted position, to warm her, and to remind her that theirs was a very passionate relationship. 'Except me,' he conceded. 'You'll grab the challenge of having a new little person in your life as you have everything else, only this time you'll have the reward of a small person who loves you as I love you. There are no quick fixes. Just trust me, and in the future you'll know I was right about you, Sadie Montgomery.'

'As you said, baby steps,' she finally accepted with a rueful smile.

'Plus time, and a lot of loving,' he said as he brought her back into his arms.

They returned in high spirits. Annalisa was at the flamenco camp with Marissa where she would stay until the heat created by her break-up with the Prince died down. Instead of interfering, as he usually did, he had taken Sadie's advice and backed off. Annalisa was safe with friends and family in the mountains, which left him free to suggest to Sadie that they should return to Madrid so she could have a doctor check her out, and stay on for a few days at his house in the city. He wanted her to know that his feelings for her wouldn't change whether he was the Gypsy King, or a member of the Spanish aristocracy.

There was no denying the fact that his life was very different in Madrid, but Sadie was adaptable, and if she wanted this as much as he did, she would accept the compromises they would both have to make. His free time would be limited, but so would hers, and when the baby came they would both have to make changes.

With so many things yet to be settled between them, they slept this last night in the mountains in each other's arms. He loved this woman and knew now that it was his responsibility to prove that he did with more than words.

The next day they arrived back at his house in Madrid.

'I'm surprised,' Sadie exclaimed as he entered the large, formal drawing room to find her waiting for him.

'By what?' he queried, thinking how beautiful she looked, with the natural grace of a duchess and the composure that said, finally, she felt secure, and that fun element that was pure, unadulterated Sadie.

'I'm surprised to see you looking so relaxed here,' she explained as he raked his shower-damp hair. 'I've only seen you dressed down like this in the mountains before.'

He noticed her cheeks pinking up as her gaze skittered over him. 'I don't wear a suit every day in the city,' he explained. 'Can I get you a drink? Water? Juice?'

'Water, please. You're usually so stiff and proper in the city,' she went on as he handed over a crystal glass of sparkling water.

He drew his head back. 'Is that how you see me? Am I really so pompous?'

'Not pompous,' she argued, frowning. 'More distant and aloof.'

'Preoccupied,' he allowed, 'but this time, I've put a hold on my diary. As you pointed out, Annalisa needs a chance to sort out her life without my interference. I can see now that solutions that might work for me wouldn't work for my sister.'

'Like punching the Prince's lights out?' Sadie suggested with her tongue firmly planted in her cheek.

He laughed. 'Don't tempt me,' he said as he opened the French doors onto the gardens.

'This is beautiful,' she said as she walked outside.

'But it all lacks a magic touch,' he said, coming up behind her. 'And that's where you come in.'

'Do I have a free hand?'

'I don't know,' he murmured, his gaze dropping to her lips. 'Do you?'

She proved it, and within a few moments they were tangling on the sofa.

'Oh, *yes*! Please,' she begged as he stripped and arranged Sadie as he wanted her, on the very edge of the firm cushions. Kneeling between her legs, he spread her wide and took her deep. The first stroke was enough to take her over the edge, and he maintained a steady rhythm until she was ready to start again.

'Don't wait this time,' she whispered. 'Come with me.'

With her powerful inner muscles clenched around him, he had no option, and with a roar of satisfaction, he staked his claim to the only woman he had ever wanted with such a fierce and overwhelming love. When at last she was quiet, he kissed her deeply and tenderly, firm in the belief that the family he had always longed to recreate was at last within his grasp.

CHAPTER SIXTEEN

IF MADRID WAS exciting at night, it was a goddess by day. Discovering the back streets, and understanding the majestic buildings with Alejandro as tour guide, was something else. Having promised to make good on his declaration of love by wooing her properly, his method of choice, to Sadie's delight and surprise, was an open-top bus, and a sweet, crispy cone, dripping with a double scoop of chocolate ice cream. Making love came naturally, he had explained, it was just the rest of the process he was battling to get his head around.

'Process?' Sadie had demanded with a frown.

'My romancing technique needs brushing up,' Alejandro had admitted, 'so I'm trying to make amends.'

While she was still trying to get over the

fact he'd said he loved her. Her biggest fear was that Alejandro loved sex and the banter between them and had mistaken that for love. Well, today, her concern would be proved or disproved, and at least there were no billionaire trappings in sight to suggest he was trying to overwhelm her with material incentives.

'Marks out of ten for this first idea?' he enquired as the engine beneath her seat began to rumble.

'Ten for the surprise factor,' she exclaimed, licking the cone furiously as her ice cream began to melt. 'Are you going to help me with this?'

Alejandro's answer was to kiss the ice cream from her lips while the cone continued to drip. 'Two for practical skills,' she scolded as he grinned and kissed her again. 'Though there are certain areas where I would award you several gold stars for your practical skills.'

If this was a lesson in ramping up sexual tension she should award him a gold star right now. 'You score a one as a tour guide,' she said as the bus stopped again. 'This is the third stop, and I'm still waiting for your commentary.'

'You taste great,' he said, 'but I prefer vanilla.'

'Since when?' she teased. Big mistake. The sexual heat that had been snapping between them now threatened to turn into an inferno.

'Are you hungry?' he asked.

'A little,' she murmured, her gaze drawn to the sharp black stubble already shading his face. And his lips…

'Only a little?' he queried, distracting her.

'Where can we…?'

'Be alone?' Alejandro slanted a sideways smile as he anticipated her question. 'Next stop.'

'A walk through the park?' Sadie queried, as they climbed down the stairs when the bus swayed to a juddering halt.

Her heart thumped with an irregular beat as Alejandro pushed his sunglasses back on his mop of black hair, revealing his thoughts quite clearly. There would be no informative commentaries on the city's history, and this would be no ordinary walk in the park.

Her pulse throbbed with anticipation as they set off, side by side, hands relaxed, but not touching. Their fingers were so tantalisingly close that it ramped up the sexual tension even more, and that expression on Alejandro's face was decidedly sensual.

'The sunsets here are legendary,' he explained as they entered the park.

'What a pity that we won't be here to see it.'

When Alejandro said nothing, she prompted him. 'Surely we won't be staying in the park until sunset?'

'Who knows? There's an ancient temple, said to have a special energy. We should try it out.'

'On our first date?' she said, pretending to be scandalised.

'Then, there's no option but to go back to the house,' he said. 'Don't worry. Our tour is merely postponed, not cancelled.'

He needed this time with Sadie, Alejandro mused as they returned to a building he had always thought impressive before, but which now seemed more like a museum than a comfortable home. They were learning so much about each other, and she was right in saying he was more relaxed than he had ever been in the city. Spending time with Sadie had given him the chance to look at things clearly, and to realise just how much was missing from his gilded life. His high-end property in a part of the city that housed some of the most expensive real estate in the world was a palace, not a home, and the old building was in desperate need of a beating heart. Sadie could provide that. He loved the fast-growing warmth and understanding between them. The question was, could he build on that?

'There's a swimming pool on the roof overlooking the city,' he said, longing suddenly for shade and cooling water.

'You've got everything here,' she commented with amazement.

And nothing, he thought. Even in the short time she'd been in residence, Sadie had transferred some of her lustre to the building. Seeing it through her eyes only proved it needed more softening touches. Leaving everything to designers had left him with an impressive, though impersonal dwelling, when what he longed for more than anything else was a home.

'No one could accuse you of doing anything by halves,' she said, smiling as she turned to face him.

'I try not to,' he agreed, wondering how a long drawn-out wooing process suited anyone. It didn't suit him. 'I'll show you around properly later,' he said—much, *much* later.

'Alejandro!' Sadie gasped as he caught her around the waist when they were only halfway up the stairs.

'Alejandro, what?' he demanded as he carefully pressed her down.

She was laughing as she asked him, 'What are you doing?'

'I'm a patient man, but I'm not a saint, and I've given the staff the day off.'

Deftly stripping her, he nudged his thigh between her legs.

Sadie's thoughts were lost in a noisy gasp of shock and pleasure. 'You are impossible.'

'But not unachievable.'

She laughed as she pulled him close. 'Don't ever stop being you,' she said.

He did his best to fulfil this request, and they didn't get dressed for a week.

Cooking for lovers would be her first cookbook, Sadie told him as they feasted on strawberries and pizza in bed. 'So, you'll give up your work at El Gato Feroz?' he queried.

'No,' she said in a tone of bemusement. 'Of course not. It's what I do.'

'What about the baby?'

Tension reared its ugly head. Grabbing a robe, Sadie told him in no uncertain manner, 'Like every other working mother, I'll sort it out.'

'But I can provide for you. You don't have to work another day in your life, if you don't want to.'

'I could just ask you for money? Is that supposed to reassure me, entice me?' Shaking her head, she sounded disappointed when she told him softly, 'You don't know me yet.'

'Yes I do,' he argued, swinging out of bed and tugging on his jeans. 'You want to work.

You have a career to pursue. No one under-
stands a strong work ethic more than me. I'm
suggesting a partnership. Marry me. Live with
me. Love me. Let's make a family together.'

'Are you serious?'

'Never more so,' he said.

'Is that a proposal?'

'Sounded like one to me.' And he had never
been more certain about anything in his life.

She was quiet for quite a while, and he knew
she was struggling with the fact that she had
nothing happy to draw on when it came to the
notion of family, while he had enjoyed everything possible to convince him that this was
right...that they were right together.

'Chef Sorollo invited you to take a sabbatical
for a very good reason,' he told Sadie gently.
'He's a family man, so he knows when you
hold that baby in your arms for the first time
you won't want to rush back to work. But that
doesn't mean the end of your career. You'll
return refreshed with lots of new ideas. Why
don't you write that cookery book you mentioned? You could dedicate it to him. Wouldn't
a good book be a boost in your profession?

You can still work, and tailor your responsibilities as a mother around that.' Far from restricting Sadie's future, he wanted her to see that in fact her life would be immeasurably improved.

'It's called balance, and I know how good you are at organisation, so getting it right should be a breeze for you.'

'A successful family,' she murmured. 'Like your parents.'

'Like my parents,' he agreed. 'You can live wherever you want to, in any one of my houses—on one condition,' he said, acting stern.

'Which is?' she demanded.

'You turn each one of them into a home. Will you do that for me?'

She stared at him for the longest time, as if she understood how lonely his gilded life had been before the woman with the flame-red hair came along to transform his thinking, and then she said, 'I will.'

His heart was like a jackhammer in his chest. It was a moment as intense as any at the altar between a bride and groom. It was a pledge for the future, and a promise he knew she wouldn't break. There was just one more thing he needed to hear her say. 'Do you trust me, Sadie? Do you trust me enough to do this?'

'I do,' she said, staring steadily into his eyes.

They went out and took that tour around the city. What they'd shared in those few precious moments after almost a week of making love was too tender and special to change gear immediately by leaping back into bed. For now it was enough to wander through the city with their fingers linked, and have Alejandro share his love of Madrid, as Sadie made silent plans to enrich his life. What Alejandro had done for her was unquantifiable, and she wanted nothing more than to make him happy. He'd freed her from doubt and trust issues, which was like being reborn into a new, brighter world. Sharing everything, as he had suggested, was a dream come true, and what she wanted most of all was that Alejandro would have the chance to enjoy his family.

His family. Glancing up, she marvelled at the force of her love, for him, and for their child.

* * *

'I've got something for you,' he told Sadie, surprising her as they stopped at a pavement café for a cooling glass of water.

'For me?' she exclaimed.

'This might not be the most romantic moment,' he said, holding a chair for her to sit down, 'but at least I've got your full attention.'

'You've had that for the best part of a week,' she admitted with a loving grin. 'What is it?' she asked as he offered his closed fist.

'Why don't you peel my fingers open and see?'

Sadie pulled a comic face as she did so and held up a key. 'The key to your heart?' she suggested lightly.

'The key to my *palacio* in Madrid,' he explained.

She looked shocked. 'I don't need this.'

'I know you don't,' he said, closing her hand around the key. 'But I want you to have it so you always feel secure.'

'It's too much.'

'It isn't enough. It could never be enough,'

he argued. 'And the *palacio* is just your first project, by the way.'

'I love a man who puts conditions on a contract.'

'Then, you've found the right man.

'So, you really want to marry me?' she said.

'Haven't I already said so? I need someone to sort out those houses of mine.'

'Then, I suppose I'd better give you a formal reply.' Her grin was infectious.

'You better had, because the *palacio* is my wedding gift to you. Did I mention that I'd like us to get married next month?'

'So soon?' Sadie queried with surprise.

'What?' he said, acting shocked. 'Won't you have time to organise the catering?'

Sadie frowned. 'I suppose I—'

'Chef Sorollo has it all in hand,' he reassured her.

'Chef Sorollo is in on this?'

He shrugged. 'You, of all people, should know the best chefs are booked up months in advance.'

'What about the best wives?'

'They have to be snapped up. And it might

interest you to know that Chef Sorollo has asked me to test the water when it comes to him giving you away.'

'Really? He'd do that?' Tears rushed to Sadie's eyes.

'Only giving you away temporarily, he told me, as he would like to offer you another position in his kitchens when you return from your sabbatical, that of planning the menus, and supervising the hiring of staff, as well as taking an interest in the new restaurant chain he plans to open...of which you will be an equal partner, of course.'

'What?'

'It gives you more time at home with the baby. You can work flexible hours to suit yourself, and it's a big step up in your career.'

'You did this,' she accused, and as she stared at him he realised he'd gone too far. 'How else could I become a partner?' she said, tensing as she added, 'I can't take your money.'

He shook his head. 'Billionaires must be allowed to lavish a few indulgences on the woman they love more than anything else in the world.'

'A few indulgences?' Sadie exclaimed. 'A *palacio* and a share in a business, all in one and the same day?'

'Fair exchange for a lifetime of love, I'd call it,' he said.

'What about the scandal when Don Alejandro, the most eligible bachelor in Spain, the infamous Duque de Alegon, marries Sadie Montgomery, a cook from a small town in England?'

'Firstly, you're not *just* a cook, you're the most amazing woman, and I don't care where you're from, and neither should you, or anyone else, for that matter. I certainly don't subscribe to the idea that inheriting a title grants me any special privileges or should command instant respect. Respect has to be earned, by dukes the same as anyone else, and from what I can see you've earned respect ten times over. And as for any so-called scandal…my father was said to have scandalised society when he married my mother, but that didn't stop him living happily with the woman he loved. My parents proved everyone wrong. Even though my mother left the freedom of the mountains for the restrictions of political and court life in Madrid, she still took my father back to the mountains from time to time. And those who are impressed by my title might be interested to know that I was both conceived and born in a caravan. One thing's for certain. Our children won't be raised with narrow boundaries, or groundless preconceptions about other people.'

'Children?' Sadie queried.

'Why not? We'll bring them up with the broadest possible horizons, so they can benefit from all the variety the world has to offer. I love you, Sadie. I love you with all my heart.' And he would reassure her every day of her life, if he had to, though something told him Sadie had turned a corner and was starting to trust him as he trusted her.

They'd both changed so much, he reflected as they kissed so tenderly and for so long that they got a round of applause from their fellow diners. He'd been accustomed to doing things his way for so many years, he couldn't remember a challenge until Sadie came into his life. He'd taken privilege for granted and had barely appreciated the sacrifices his parents had made. His mother, giving up her freedom in the mountains to raise him as the son of a duke, and his father laying the foundations of a successful business that brought prosperity to countless families, and yet still finding time to be at home with his son. What a heritage to pass on to his children. His only wish was to continue that rich tradition of loyalty, support and love, and he was confident that with Sadie at his side the legacy would continue. Between them they would introduce their child to both sides of its heritage, and there was not one iota of doubt in his mind that Sadie would be the most wonderful mother.

'Thankfully, I've come prepared,' he said as they left the café.

'What do you mean?' she asked as he stopped beside one of Madrid's most beautiful fountains. Dipping down onto one knee, he held up a diamond solitaire that glittered with all the colours of the rainbow. 'Will you marry me, Sadie Montgomery? Will you make me the happiest man on earth?'

'I can't accept that,' she exclaimed as she looked at the ring.

'You can,' he told her.

'Okay, I will,' she said, her eyes sparkling with laughter and love. 'One *palacio*, a partnership in a business and now a diamond ring… I could get used to this sort of thing.'

'You're going to have to,' he said. 'Always and for ever, Sadie,' he murmured, kissing her palm before slipping the sparkling diamond ring on her ring finger.

As he sprang to his feet, he became aware that a crowd had gathered, and everyone was cheering. 'Always and for ever,' Sadie repeated in a whisper as he drew the woman he loved into his arms for a kiss.

EPILOGUE

PEOPLE ACROSS THE world hailed the marriage between Sadie Montgomery and Alejandro, Duque de Alegon as the most romantic wedding of the year. At Sadie's wish, the celebration was held in Alejandro's private chapel deep in the Sierra Nevada, rather than in Madrid. His power and magnetism were such that, when the invitations went out, politicians, royals and celebrities alike simply shrugged and packed their bags for an unusual wedding in the mountains between an aristocratic Spanish duke, whom the press had dubbed the Gypsy King, and a girl from a small town, who would have no immediate family at the wedding. But Sadie had invited all the friends she had made since meeting Alejandro, and, of course, Chef Sorollo, the man who had played such an important part in her life and who would continue to do so, took a leading role. Sadie wanted the people she cared about to join her on this happiest of days.

The choir was sublime, the ceremony was magical, and everyone agreed that the bride's dress, with its overlay of finest Swiss lace, was the most ravishing bridal gown they'd ever seen. With a demure neckline, three-quarter sleeves, and a subtle skirt that fell to the ground in elegant waves of silk, it was designed to be removed easily, so the bride could change for the evening without much trouble. Or so Alejandro would have no trouble removing it, Sadie thought as she smiled a secret smile. A most fabulous tulle veil billowed for twenty feet behind her and was secured with an Alegon family diamond tiara that glittered and flashed at the slightest movement of her head. Alejandro had requested that Sadie wear her hair loose, so it cascaded to her waist in a fiery mane of glossy red waves.

She walked up the aisle on the arm of Chef Sorollo, with Annalisa, Marissa and Maria as her attendants. The bride was so radiant with happiness that everyone applauded. The chapel was full of the most exquisitely scented blooms. After the formal ceremony, a party in the evening would be a feast of flamenco at a real flamenco camp, to honour the noble Duke's heritage. An air of excitement had gripped all the guests since the moment the invitations went out, for while the wedding itself would be stately and gracious, as befitted a Spanish grandee, the evening party promised to be very different.

When Sadie reached Alejandro's side in the chapel, he turned to exclaim, 'You're so beautiful. You look incredible. And I love you so much...'

Sadie was beyond words as she stared into Alejandro's eyes. He was off-the-scale handsome in a sharp black uniform that set off his darkly glittering saturnine glamour to perfection. A sash to denote his rank, made of ruby-red silk, ran diagonally across the impressive width of his muscular chest, and was secured on his breast by a fabulous glittering jewel. Sadie had to remind herself that this man was the father of her child, and, improbable though it might seem, he loved her unconditionally.

She was mesmerised by Alejandro, by his compelling presence, and the beauty of his eyes when he dipped his head to confide something in her ear.

'I'll have you in half an hour,' he whispered.

'Alejandro!' she whispered back while the choir's voices rose in a solemn anthem. 'How am I supposed to concentrate on the ceremony now?'

'You're not,' he said, with a shrug and a smile that quirked his firm, sensuous lips. 'Just remember to say "I do" at the appropriate moment.'

'But, half an hour?' Sadie queried as the congregation settled down.

'It will take that long for everyone to be seated for the wedding breakfast,' Alejandro explained with a nonchalant shrug, 'during which time the bride and groom will be otherwise occupied, though we will join our guests later.'

'Okay,' she whispered, silencing him. 'I don't need to hear that now.'

Fortunately, they were called upon to pay attention to the service, though Alejandro's faint smile suggested he hadn't forgotten his promise, that when everyone else was enjoying a welcoming glass of champagne, the bride and groom would be enjoying each other.

What a striking couple they made, people said as the swarthy Duke, so tall and stern, left the chapel with his tiny, spirited bride to find horses waiting for them outside. Now she noticed that he was wearing tight black breeches beneath his formal jacket. Still laughing at her surprise, he sprang into the saddle and, reaching down, he brought her in front of him. Deftly arranging the yards of tulle and silk, he shortened the reins and they were off. Cheers echoed behind them as Alejandro held her close.

'We've got a head start on our guests,' he exulted, 'so that gives us even longer than I imagined, and I intend to make full use of every extra second.'

Within a few short minutes, or so it seemed to Sadie, he reined in beside a familiar caravan. 'Your bed awaits, Duquesa.'

And so did her lover, Sadie thought, breathless with excitement as Alejandro bounded up the steps.

The bride and groom were extremely late for their party. The flamenco dancers were already well into their performance, but the moment that Alejandro appeared hand in hand with his bride, a hush fell over the assembled guests.

'Your Majesties, lords, ladies and gentlemen,' Alejandro announced, 'May I introduce my beautiful bride…?'

A collective sigh of surprise and appreciation rose amongst the guests as they took in the sight of the imperious Spanish Duke, backed by a blazing campfire, dressed all in black with a sash around his waist, his swarthy face as proud as any gypsy king, and his young bride, her glorious auburn hair flying free as she danced in his arms wearing a pure white flamenco gown.

'Dance,' Alejandro invited their awestruck audience, once he and Sadie had finished the traditional first dance. They retired from the dance floor to a thunder of applause. 'And may the heart of old Spain guide your footsteps,' he called out as he led his bride away.

'As it guided mine,' Sadie said as she stared at Alejandro.

'We were always meant to be together,' he said. 'It was merely a matter of time before you accepted the inevitable.'

'And you accepted that you can't have everything your own way,' she countered.

'I can have you any way I want.'

'You might be right where that's concerned,' Sadie agreed, shooting a smile at Alejandro. This was one occasion when she had no intention of entering into a heated discussion with him, as there were far more important things for them to do.

* * * * *

LET'S TALK

Romance

For exclusive extracts, competitions
and special offers, find us online:

f facebook.com/millsandboon

⊙ @millsandboonuk

𝕪 @millsandboon

Or get in touch on 0844 844 1351*

For all the latest titles coming soon,
visit millsandboon.co.uk/nextmonth

*Calls cost 7p per minute plus your phone company's price per
minute access charge